Buck Falaya

James Killgore

Polygon
Edinburgh

For Ann

© James Killgore 1995

Published by
Polygon
22 George Square
Edinburgh

Set in Palatino by Bibliocraft, Dundee
and printed and bound in Great Britain by
Short Run Press Ltd, Exeter

A CIP record for this title is available

The right of James Killgore to be identified as the author of this work
has been asserted by him in accordance with the Copyright, Designs and
Patents Act 1988.

ISBN 0 7486 6194 8

The Publisher acknowledges subsidy from

THE SCOTTISH ARTS COUNCIL

towards the publication of this volume.

Chapter 1

It's not as though my brother was particularly fond of animals. He was not the sort of kid to loiter at pet shop windows, or bring home bluejay hatchlings in a shoe box. In truth, before his beloved Traveller, the only time I can recall Rankin showing any interest at all in nature was when he was about eleven. He took up with a fledgling sociopath named Claude Glass, who lived a few doors down from our house on Franklin Place in New Orleans. That summer the pair of them set out, quite systematically, to annihilate every last reptile and amphibian in the neighborhood.

Lizards were favored victims. Often whole cabals would be hung summarily using strands of dental floss tied to gallows fashioned from bent coat hangers. The lizards would dance and jerk, professing their innocence by a certain lack of resignation. Less fortunate ones were crucified on crosses made from popsicle sticks, or burnt at the stake after being doused with Zippo lighter fluid.

Frogs caught in a culvert opening near our house became subjects in brutal experiments. Claude was a prodigy when it came to cruelty. Once I saw him inject a syringe of Dr Tichenor's Antiseptic Mouthwash into the soft underbelly of a leopard frog. The needle he'd stolen from his younger brother Frank, a pale, overprotected diabetic who I rarely saw outdoors except at school. The frog gulped once and died. But perhaps the worst scene I witnessed was the dissection of a small grass snake with a Black Cat firecracker shoved down its gullet.

Now I like to think that my brother didn't get quite the same thrill that Claude derived from these atrocities. Never once did I see Rankin actually do the killing. I think it was more the spectacle of death that fascinated him.

Each time Claude dispatched another small creature, Rankin would gather up the remains and bear them to a patch of waste ground along the railroad line which ran across the back end of our street. Here he would bury it in the dirt and mark the grave with an oyster shell filched from the back of Manchac Seafood out along Metairie Road.

Over the course of June and July this tiny potter's field grew row by row, with Rankin making improvements here and there, just like any other summer project, a model Saturn rocket or a tree house. My brother should probably have been packed off to Dr. Hardy, or at least to Father Ambrose. But his secret remained hidden. I was eight at the time and thought it best to keep silent – mainly out of fear that Claude Glass might steal into my bedroom window one night with his shiny Barlow pocket knife. But I also felt an odd sense of shame and disgust at my own curiosity, which was really a form of complicity. I still occasionally have nightmares about that tiny cemetery now long obliterated by weeds.

To be fair to my brother this was an isolated period in his life. That is to say Rankin was not a particularly twisted child, or

at least not to my mind. To meet him at age twelve you would
probably have been charmed. Certainly most people were.

Not that he was an especially good-looking kid. Grinning,
with a high square forehead thick with freckles, and small
protruding ears – this is how he appears in his seventh grade
class photograph. It's in the 1964 edition of *The Flame* – the St
Francis Xavier school annual. His thin blond hair is cut short
and plastered to his scalp with Brylcream. His teeth don't
look particularly good.

'Edward Rankin Calhoun' reads the caption beneath,
though the first name has since been scratched out with a
ball point pen. My brother hated being called Edward, or
even worse 'Ed'. Substitute teachers tended to be the worst
offenders. Once or twice he let himself be marked absent out
of pure obstinance. The name Rankin derives from a great
uncle of ours who flew in the U.S. Army Air Corps during
the early 1930s. Lt John Rankin died at twenty-four when his
Martin B-10 bomber crashed into an icy Texas hillside while
flying a mail route for the Postal Service. He had just married
my great Aunt Jean, and the only picture she has of him is
on their wedding day in 1933.

Neither did my brother distinguish himself much at school.
That was more my province. This is not to say Rankin was
dumb – far from it – just amazingly inconsistent. It wasn't
unusual for him to bring home a report card with almost
all D's and one A-plus, usually in science or geography or
whatever held his interest at the time. His teachers would
comment 'bright but lacks motivation.' My father saw it
as plain laziness. But it was just that kind of maddening
characteristic which seemed to draw people to Rankin – an
easy-going sort of honesty.

There was one single factor, however, which endeared
my brother most to adults who knew our family, to doting
aunts and school teachers, nuns and elderly friends of my

grandmother. It was also partly the source of his occasional tendency towards the morose. Rankin was motherless.

The accident in which our mother died happened when I was barely a year old. Not the faintest trace of it remains in my memory, though I was lucky to have survived myself – or so I've been told on countless occasions. Nor do I retain any living impression of my mother, just an absence. Literally when I think of her I picture an empty sunlit hall in that old house on Franklin Place. So I say Rankin was motherless, without including myself in that description.

My childhood was, for the most part, scandalously warm and secure. Some of the earliest memories I can conjure up are of soft brown hands and a pleasant eclipsing face that could grin, pucker and cajole me out of any sour mood. They belonged to a woman named Ophelia Bertrand. She sponged and cuddled and calmed me through infancy; no mother could have done more.

Ophelia must have been about twenty-one when she first came to live with us. Her family was from False River, and her mother had kept house for the Guichards, an old Creole family who still own a significant chunk of Pointe Coupee Parish. Ophelia moved to New Orleans just after her high school graduation and worked for another family Uptown before my father hired her. Back then Rankin and I knew almost nothing of her past; why she'd left home and how she'd come to look after us. I find it surprising now to think just how much we took for granted.

Our house was a brick two-story built before World War II, as were most of the houses on Franklin Place and the surrounding streets. The area is known as 'Old Metairie' – the 'Old' serving to distinguish it from greater Metairie, a huge post-war suburb of mainly salt-box houses, apartment buildings and shopping malls sprawling far out beyond Orleans Parish to the lakefront. Old Metairie has always considered itself more refined, more 'Uptown', than the rest of Metairie, though just why has never been clear to me.

The houses on Franklin Place were not particularly grand. Ours had three bedrooms, a small drab den and a rarely used dining room. At the rear of the house, with a door opening out to the backyard, was Ophelia's kitchen. Here Rankin and I ate our meals, did most of our homework and watched all of our TV. The room was dominated by a massive oak breakfast table and six frayed, wicker-back dining chairs.

Every afternoon Ophelia sat in the same chair waiting for us to come home from school – usually a cup of coffee and a Reader's Digest condensed novel on the table in front of her, the radio tuned to Sid Noel. Nearly every afternoon she and my brother performed a ritual that varied little from day to day. Rankin would appear at the kitchen door just before dinner and announce:

'I'm having a Coke.'

'No sir,' Ophelia would say, not even glancing up from her book. 'One Coke a day you done had it.'

'Come on. It won't kill me.'

'Maybe not. But it'll rot every last tooth out that empty head.'

'Well they're not your teeth. So I'm getting one anyway.'

Ophelia would glare up from her reading.

'Touch that fridge and I'll break both your thumbs.'

But Rankin would only grin and reach out and brush his fingers across the handle.

'Don't you be getting on my nerves, boy.'

Then in one quick motion he'd flick open the door and snatch out a bottle. Instantly, Ophelia would be up out of her chair in pursuit around the table.

'Put that back. Now!'

'No mam.'

'Then you best not let me catch you.'

'You too fat to catch anyone.'

'You gonna see fat in a minute – fat lip.'

'Not unless you can fly.'

'Better hope I don't for your sake.'

Two or three minutes this would go on, until eventually Ophelia would catch Rankin in a head lock and twist a clump of blond hair around her finger.

'Say it.'

'Say what?' he'd yowl.

'Say it or I'll scalp you.'

'Okay. You plug ugly.'

Ophelia would smile sweetly at me and twist her finger a little tighter.

'Did I hear right David?'

Rankin would then scream:

'I mean beautiful.'

'What was that? Speak up.'

'Ophelia Bertrand is smart and beautiful'.

'Why how kind of you to say so,' she'd coo, and then smooth his hair back into place.

Ophelia raised my brother from age four. Probably no one understood him better. But she was no mother to Rankin. 'Mother' reposed in an old oak bureau in a corner of our den. Inside the top drawer was an album full of pictures taken at a small one-storey house off Bonnabel Boulevard not far from the Lakefront. This was where my parents lived when Rankin was still a baby – before I was born.

Just as with most first children there are dozens of photos of Rankin, all taken by my father with a cheap Kodak: my mother holding a splashing Rankin in a blue plastic baby pool, Rankin crawling on the rug toward her laughing, Rankin eating dinner, his eyes huge like a bush baby's, my mother's face pushed against his cheek. In each of these photos she wears this fixed, gracious smile on her face that I've come to find vaguely irritating over the years. No denying she was a pretty woman, with long dark hair and large, green eyes. But in almost every photo her body has this posed quality, a stiffness in contrast with Rankin's infant exuberance, like some old time Louisiana politician who's breezed in to kiss a few babies.

Occasionally in the background of these pictures another figure can be seen, a small middle-aged black woman named Ruby. She came in five days a week, though surely my father could hardly have afforded a maid on his salary then. But obviously my mother needed assistance managing that small house with one baby. Besides, no self-respecting white woman in her circle of friends would be without 'help'.

Margot Frances Aubry, my mother, was born and grew up in a house on Prytania in the Garden District. Aubry is an old New Orleans name dating back before the War of 1812, prominent in the Uptown social firmament. Margot spent twelve years attending the Louise S. McGehee School for girls, just four blocks from her house.

At age eighteen she made her debut on a warm August night at Gallier Hall, with a jazz quartet and weeping ice sculptures. That Fall she started at Sophie Newcomb college, pledged Kappa Kappa Gamma, and delared Art History her major. A careful chronology of my mother's short life is kept in a leather bound album by my grandmother – report cards, photo portraits, party invitations, yellowed cuttings from the society pages of the *Times Picayune*.

My parents began dating during their senior year. My father had come to Tulane University from a small town near the Arkansas border. He grew up in a house built nearly 150 years ago by a Calhoun from Macon County, Georgia. It was a large 'hill farm' style house with only pretensions towards grandeur. Farming there during my father's childhood was strictly subsistence. Frank Calhoun was the Parish Clerk of Court, though somehow I'm sure my mother conceived of my father as a planter's son, with his creamy North Louisiana accent.

Before Margot Aubry got married she'd rarely set foot out of Uptown New Orleans. No other place could possibly matter to her, so that squat little house on Bonnabel was not going to do for long. It was just before I was born that my father bought our house in that older, more gracious quarter of Metairie.

Ruby's bus trip grew from a half hour to one and a quarter. But Margot Aubry was finally back in her element. By the time I was born, she was completely immersed in the luncheons and sanitary charities of the New Orleans Junior League.

One hot afternoon in early July my mother packed me into a portable cot and drove over to visit Gerry Whitney, an old school friend of hers who lived Uptown on Magnolia off Audubon Park. Two hours later she departed and instead of driving back to Metairie headed out along River Road toward Vacherie. No one in the family has ever been able to explain to me just what she was doing out on that broken-down highway near Edgard. But the car was not travelling fast – only 30 or 40 – when it veered off the road and hit the edge of a bridge. It flipped once and landed on its roof in the canal. All the windows were open so we sank like a stone.

Two black men fishing on the bank witnessed the scene. One dove into the brown water and felt his way blind along the hood to the passenger window. He found me first but was a few minutes too late in locating my mother. A doctor at the hospital later told my father that she must have been knocked unconscious and would have been spared any great anguish. Maybe he could have said more, but he didn't.

Death had as little meaning to Rankin at age four as it did to me. Yet he can still remember certain aspects of the funeral with amazing clarity. Just after breakfast on that day Ruby dressed him in his Sunday suit – light blue linen with short pants and a jacket sporting massive white buttons. He must have looked oddly gay next to my father's black serge.

St. Cecilia's had packed the pews that day, this being a funeral of uncommon appeal. No octogenarian banker or dowager aunt, here was a young mother torn tragically from her husband and two young boys. Father Ambrose, who had married Margot Aubry just six years before, would now bury her.

The congregation tried to be respectful, tried not to turn when my father walked into that sighing air-conditioned church, Ruby behind with my brother in hand. But the temptation was just too great. Rankin can remember people staring at him – their rigid masks of tragedy. He discovered that if he stared back into the faces, they would turn away. It seemed funny to him at the time, having this powerful effect on adults. Sorrow had cloaked and crowned him, made him somehow special.

A black limo hired from Eagan Funeral Home took them to the cemetery. A canvas marquee stood over the grave and the dirt infill was covered with a tarp and garlanded with flowers. The mourners sweated profusely, being unaccustomed to standing out of the air conditioning. Off in the distance some children were shooting off firecrackers and bottle rockets; the Fourth was only a day away.

As Father Ambrose droned his prayers over the grave, my brother became fidgety. He wanted to go and see the fireworks. Eventually he made such a fuss that Ruby had to lead him away, through the gravestones to the edge of the cemetery. Here she held his hand and they watched the hissing rockets shoot up from behind a tall hedge and crack over the rooftops.

Rankin also retains another image from that day, though he's never been quite certain it wasn't a dream. The night after the funeral he remembers waking from a nightmare and slipping out of bed to go look for our mother. He climbed down the stairs and wandered into the den. There my father sat in his armchair with all the lights off except for a single reading lamp. In his hand was a sheet of writing paper which he tore into small equal-sized pieces and dropped to the floor. He then picked up another sheet and began reading.

Rankin's appearance in the room startled him and he stood up quickly.

'What are you doing down here?'

Rankin can remember a look of sudden rage on his face though it passed in an instant. He then gathered my brother in his arms and tucked him back into bed. The significance of this memory long eluded Rankin. My father never spoke of it again – just as he rarely spoke of anything to do with the accident or our mother.

Over the years, our mother's absence, the heavy air of her death, became more palpable to my brother. Memories of the funeral began to plague him. Many nights when I was little I remember being awoken by Rankin crying in his dreams. Ophelia, newly hired to replace Ruby who had a family of her own, would slip into the room and calm him back to sleep.

Matters weren't helped much by our grandmother. Every Sunday after Mass, Rankin and I were driven to the house on Prytania for a visit. First we'd have lunch and then Big Mum would sit us in her parlour and bring out my mother's old photo albums and scrapbooks. Big Mum was determined that we should never doubt just how pure and faultless her daughter had been. An old crystal Waterford clock on the mantle would tick away the hours of catechism.

'You know your mother was a brillant reader at your age, Rankin,' she'd say.

'Louisa May Alcott and the Brontës. Sometimes I wonder if she would have written a book herself. At McGehee's, she made up lovely, funny little poems. I can remember one about Jack, the colored man who used to do the yard.'

Out would come old report cards, copy books, wrinkled water color sketches, Margot's first communion Bible and lace – Big Mum had saved it all. Then, inevitably, she would remind us to pray to our mother, as she did, asking her to intercede for us with all the saints in Heaven.

'Your mother looks down over us every moment of the day,' Big Mum would say, adding how this gave her great comfort. To me it seemed a spooky thought; to Rankin approaching age thirteen it must have been no less than chilling.

Perhaps I'm too hard on Big Mum. The death of her daughter was to me history long past. But Big Mum seemed unable to move beyond that event in time: she lived always with the immediacy of it, up to the very day of her own death.

This did nothing, however, to help my brother get over his loss. Rankin idealized our mother out of all proportion, as did I though perhaps with less conviction. He believed everything Big Mum said. That beautiful face in those photographs held a sort of painful promise, forever denied to him.

So I suppose it's not surprising that my brother was a little obsessed with death. Though that summer with Claude Glass it verged on a sickness. I think Rankin realised as much. He grew increasingly tense and irritable. July was never a pleasant month for him anyway. The heat and the crack of fireworks, the very smell of the warm earth seemed to bring him back to that sweltering graveside years before.

Ophelia was lucky to get more than a word or two out of Rankin. He'd disappear after breakfast and would not show up again until dinner. Then afterwards he'd sit in silence in front of the TV until bedtime.

For the first few mornings that summer I tried to follow him to Claude's house. But once out the door Rankin would grab my collar and whisper:

'Beat it, Milo.'

Milo was Rankin's nickname for me, and I hated it beyond reason. The real Milo was a cartoon monkey out of a vapid picture book given to me by my grandmother. In the book this monkey is taken from the jungle and adopted by an Park Avenue widow who dresses it up like a little boy. But Milo escapes and gets chased through New York City before being rescued by a traffic cop on the end of a flag pole at the top of the Empire State Building. Big Mum was forever insisting that I read the book out loud. Rankin soon found that he could win any argument just by chanting 'Baby Milo escapes' – which would drive me into a senseless rage.

But by age eight I'd grown somewhat thicker-skinned. I remember telling Rankin that he could not legally stop me following him, seeing as he didn't own the yard or the sidewalk or the street. To which he'd counter:

'But I can punch your face in.'

This was when I decided to make a game out of spying on him and Claude. Near the waste ground along the railroad tracks where they carried out most of their executions was a giant unpruned ligustrum hedge, almost tree-sized. Climbing up among the high branches I found a hidden vantage point from which I could watch the two using my father's Army Surplus field binoculars. Rankin always suspected I was there and would occasionally shout threats. But Claude rarely looked up from whatever atrocity was underway.

Claude was a tall gangly kid, with lank blond hair and slate blue eyes. His father was a city councillor and sent him to a Jesuit boarding school in Mississippi where the Brothers had the reputation for 'beating in' discipline. Far as I could tell it seemed only to make Claude that much more sadistic. I was just thankful they kept him locked up most of the year.

Day after day that summer I observed this two-boy pogrom in action – at least until one afternoon in late July. I remember having watched for nearly an hour as Claude used a magnifying glass to sear the flesh off a small, struggling toad. It was a blistering hot day. My leg was wedged in an awkward spot between two branches and had gone completely numb. I lowered the binoculars and tried to shift positions. But as I braced my weight against one of the branches there was a sharp crack and I found myself tumbling down through the foliage.

I landed heavily at the base of the hedge, in full view of Claude and my brother. Both of them looked up in genuine surprise. But when Claude caught sight of me sprawled there in the dirt – a potential witness – he was up and running in an instant. I scrambled frantically back through the hedge to the sidewalk on the other side, my leg still dead and useless. Claude crashed into the ligustrum and was hung up momentarily in the thick branches. This gave me time to regain my feet and propel myself down the pavement. I moved with surprising speed, throwing my paralysed limb down the sidewalk like an old wooden prosthesis.

Claude broke free of the hedge and bounded after me. Rankin emerged a few paces behind him, probably less interested in catching me than in being there when Claude did. By that point I was only a half block from the house. Then, to my horror, I heard a low growl off to the right and turned to find Dotty Wingfield's two miniature collies racing across the grass towards me. Huntley and Brinkley were the scourge of bicyclists and skaters in our neighborhood, seeing us all, I suppose, as so many renegade sheep. But luckily it was Claude who appealed to their herding instinct that day. They bore down on him, yapping and nipping at his ankles. He began to curse and kick at the dogs. I took my chance then, dashing between two parked cars, across the street and up our driveway.

Ophelia was out hanging sheets when I burst through the gate into the backyard and dropped, gasping, onto the grass. Only then did I look back to find Claude peering over the fence. Rankin was nowhere to be seen.

'What's that creepy boy want with you?' Ophelia asked.

'Nothing. We were just messing around.'

'Messing around, huh? Looks more serious than that to

me,' she said, and gathered up her basket to go back into the house.

'Wish ya'll'd find some nice friends.'

Later that night Rankin told me that Claude was now out to get me. He'd said I was to be executed as a foreign spy – a not-so-childish threat considering the guy's record. It was certainly enough to keep me confined to the yard. For the next week I moped in and out of the kitchen with this or that toy or comic. Ophelia eventually grew tired of having me always under her feet.

'Don't you have some place else in this neighborhood to play?' she asked.

'But I like it here with my own stuff.'

In truth I was miserably bored.

'Maybe I could ask Peter over to spend the night.'

'That's not exactly what I had in mind,' said Ophelia.

But she agreed, and the next morning I phoned Peter Owens, my best friend from school. Peter lived a few miles up Metairie Road near Orleans Country Club. He was the smartest kid in my class at St. Francis. Dr. Owens was a heart surgeon at Ochsner's and demanded nothing less than straight 'A's from his son. Kids at school called Peter 'stick insect' because of his small, spindly body and oversized head. Match this with a quiet intensity – mostly due to shyness – and Peter made the perfect victim. But he took the abuse stoically, seeming to know even at age eight just how far he'd someday outstrip his tormentors.

Mrs. Owens dropped Peter off at the house for lunch. Later that afternoon I filled my old plastic baby pool with water from the hose. We changed into our bathing suits and sat in the pool to cool off. That's when I told him about the miniature graveyard. Peter was fascinated.

'Boy I'd give anything to see that,' he said.

Rankin had earlier asked Ophelia if he and Claude could

go up to McNulty's to buy comic books. It seemed safe enough for us to have a quick look. So we slipped into our sneakers and ran down to the railroad tracks, still wearing our suits.

Claude and Rankin were nowhere in sight.

'It's just over there,' I whispered, pointing from the edge of the bushes.

'I can't see nothing. Let's get closer.'

Without warning Peter dashed out from behind me and across the railroad tracks.

'Wait,' I hissed.

But he was already running low through the weeds towards the waste ground. I clenched my teeth and followed. Nothing happened. I ran along the tracks to where Peter stood, gazing down at his feet.

It was the first time I'd seen Rankin's project at close view – a small square plot bordered neatly with crumbling bricks. Perhaps fifty tiny graves were laid out in rows, each marked with an oyster shell, the mother-of-pearl upright, white and vitreous like marble. A small plastic statue of Jesus – a confirmation gift – stood on one of the bricks behind the graves, his arms open in benediction. Rankin had paid attention to the smallest details, a wide drive for the miniature hearse, pebble-lined paths for the mourners.

I crouched down to take a closer look. Just at that very moment a brick sailed over my shoulder and mowed down a row of shells. My heart stopped. I swung around. But it was only Peter there. He was bending over to pick up another brick. This one bounced over the ground and levelled Jesus off his pedestal. First I thought to stop him, but instead I reached for a brick.

I can't say if it was out of pure destructiveness, or some childish sense of justice. But we wiped out my brother's cemetery in less than a minute and raced off in terror expecting Claude Glass to catch us at any moment and cut our throats.

Later that night after dinner Peter and I were upstairs

playing cards. He had been trying to teach me bridge: the
Owens family played every Sunday night. But I'd found the
scoring too complicated and we'd settled for a game of Gin
Rummy. Rankin had gone out just after dinner. I'd spent
most of the meal hoping he couldn't read the guilt written
across my face.

An hour or so later I heard the kitchen door slam and my
brother's footsteps on the stairs. My back was to the door
when he came quietly into the bedroom. Peter glanced up
from his Gin hand with an uneasy smile. Then I felt a hand
grip the back of my collar and the bed seemed suddenly to
rise up into my face. The playing cards scattered across the
floor and Peter dived for the closet. Rankin flipped me onto
my back and began punching – wild blows to the face which
I tried to block with my arms. A high-pitched buzzing filled
my ears. Blood began to stream from my nose. But more than
the pain, it was the violence that upset me most, the hatred in
his face. I remember not being able to cry – my mouth open
but the sound choked and cut off.

Then, just as suddenly as he'd begun, Rankin backed off
and retreated to the door. He looked almost as shocked as
I was, gasping for breath. I climbed off the bed and tried to
push past him out of the room. But he grabbed my shoulders.

'Don't tell Ophelia,' he whispered. 'She'll kill me. I swear
I'll never touch you again. I swear.'

He then let go of my shoulders and leaned back against
the door, his arms hanging limp.

'Come on. You punch me anywhere. Punch me in the face.
I won't hit back. Come on – I deserve it.'

But I just stood there crying, blood and snot running over
my chin. So Rankin began to punch himself, pounding his
arms and thighs until they were bright red.

'Come on. God dammit.'

Chapter 2

It was a turn in my father's fortunes in the oil business that first brought us to Buck Falaya in 1965. By then George Calhoun had worked as an exploration geologist at Kerr-McGee for nearly fourteen years. In that time he'd analysed hundreds of seismic lines, correlated the electric logs of countless drilling wells throughout southern Louisiana – his efforts yielding more than two dozen productive oil and gas wells, along with a field discovery south of Lake Charles in Cameron Parish.

But as a company geologist these finds earned my father little more than a slap on the back. So that year he decided to strike out on his own as an independent. Two attorneys who specialized in oil lease brokerage set him up with a retainer's fee in a small office in the Cress Building downtown. It was quite a gamble.

Over the next year he made a quick survey of a number of fields in south-central Louisiana and eventually came up with a couple of prospects which the attorneys leased and turned over to a small drilling company called Delphi Petroleum. My father earned a finder's fee along with a royalty and working interest in any productive wells.

One of the prospects was in Evangeline Parish, at a small town called Sweetgum. A few years ago I drove through the place out of curiosity – a drab mainstreet with a single traffic light, rusting grain silo, a few sad box houses, all surrounded by a flat expanse of rice and alfalpha. Just west of the town was a small oil field with a productive sandstone formation at about five thousand feet. My father managed to relate that formation to a deeper geologic structure directly under Sweetgum. A well drilled that July in an abandoned lot next to the town cemetery sunk pipe into a rich oil reservoir, pumping over 400 barrels in just the first day.

Sweetgum field gushed for years. I still get royalty checks, though they've now shrunk to only a few dollars a month, barely enough to treat myself to a hamburger. But in 1964 my father found himself, if not rich, squarely well off. The news caught him off-guard, sort of like an intense long-distance swimmer who lifts his head from the water at the end of a race only to find his competition just pushing off the far wall. Suddenly he was way ahead of the game, secure enough to ease off a little.

'Enjoy life, get to know my sons,' is how I imagine him explaining it to his lunch partners at the Petroleum Club. Certainly, Rankin and I then knew our father little better than our mother long in the ground.

Working at Kerr-McGee he'd kept late hours, usually arriving home long after dinner. In the mornings he'd leave the house before seven a.m. We saw even less of him as an independent.

Most Saturdays he spent at his office downtown – two rooms on the eleventh floor overlooking South Rampart Street. The small outer office was empty but for an old mahogany coat-stand and a broken swivel desk-chair. The inner office where my father worked was so crowded with paper there was hardly room to stand. Stacks of well logs lined the walls and teetered off the tops of filing cabinets. A large drafting table stood in the centre of the room, buried in contour maps and geologic cross sections and sheets of yellow legal paper crowded with working sketches and production figures. On one wall hung a large photograph of my father's first offshore well – a drilling platform at night, sparkling like a Christmas tree with green and red lights. Otherwise there were no other personal mementos, no family photographs, nothing frivolous or less than abstract. Here George Calhoun abandoned himself to business.

My father's main contribution to our day-to-day upbringing was through a series of edicts issued hurriedly each morning at the front door. Ophelia's voice would filter back through to the kitchen,

'Yes, Mr. Calhoun . . . Oh, I see they will. Two hours TV. Yes sir.'

Ophelia would then promptly ignore everything he told her and run the household in the best way she saw fit. So even indirect contact was cut off. But I can't say my father ignored us all together. Once every month or so he would pack Rankin and me into the Oldsmobile and drive us downtown to Steimel's Barbershop in the lobby of the Whitney Bank Building. My father looked on this as tradition. Back in the 1930s his father used to take him into the small town of Carthage every Saturday morning for a haircut – a rowdy cottonbelt barbershop full of gossip and cigar smoke.

Saturdays at Steimel's bore no resemblance to this, the only customers being a few lonely and obsessive business-men. We usually had the shop to ourselves and Lloyd the barber would take us each in turn as my father had his shoes shined and read the *Wall Street Journal*. Never once did Lloyd – a large, round-shouldered sloth-like man whose breath stank of cigarettes and Listerine – ask us how we wanted our hair cut. He took orders only from George.

Now I didn't mind these trips downtown so much – a few unpleasant moments in the barber chair and then a catfish po'boy for lunch at Darby's. But my brother hated them. For reasons never quite certain to me Rankin always managed to somehow irritate my father. Nothing he said or did seemed to be a particular cause. He was never flippant or disrespectful – at least not within hearing. He did everything expected of him. Throughout Junior High Rankin played on the football team, though most games he spent on the bench with 'the rest of the girls' as Coach Peters called the second and third string. Each Thursday night he went to Boy Scouts and struggled half-heartedly for merit badges, barely making it beyond Tenderfoot. Even at school he didn't do badly. But it was never enough for my father.

George Calhoun had always been an achiever – Eagle Scout, halfback on the football team at Lyndon High, salutatorian of his graduating class. Even at Tulane he apparently spent most of his time studying in the library.

Gerry Whitney called him the 'Geologic Bore'. I read this once in a postcard I found in a box of my mother's letters up in the attic. Gerry sent it from Rome while on her 'grand tour' of Europe after graduating from Newcomb. This must have been just before my parents got married. Gerry was to be the maid of honor and had written:

'Got your letter. You are such a mess Franie (her nickname for my mother). Just stick with old George. He'll put some rocks in your pockets – keep you from floating off into the ether. Never know, he might one day strike a gusher like J Paul Getty. You can be sure that Hollis couldn't find oil in an Esso station.'

This was the first time I had seen the name Hollis, but I won't go into that just now.

George expected the same level of dedication and seriousness in his sons – though I never felt quite as much pressure as Rankin. My father had little to complain about my efforts, at least academically. My report cards were numbingly perfect. I didn't make my first B until I was in the fifth grade. It was in Physical Education. I couldn't manage five pull-ups for Coach Peters. This was the sole reason for my failure and I cried bitterly over it. (That same night, I recall, Rankin did twenty pulls-ups on the shower bar as I brushed my teeth.)

Maybe it was because Rankin was older – the first born – but there was something else between him and my father, an unspoken enmity present for as long as I could remember, always shunting them apart like the positive poles of two magnets. It made my brother wary, and seemed to bring out an arbitrary vindictiveness in my father.

There was one time I recall when a few months had passed between our last visit to Steimel's. Rankin's hair was very straight and his bangs had grown a couple of inches down over his forehead – nothing radical by 1965 standards. But my father was outraged once he'd noticed.

'You ever seen hair like that on a boy?' he asked Lloyd when it was Rankin's turn in the chair.

'See much worse than that on TV, Mr. Calhoun. Like they trying to put us barbers out of business.'

Lloyd had cut my father's hair every two weeks for the last fifteen years in a style unchanged from 1953. A few years later I remember he hung a sign over his chair: 'No hippies or homosexuals'. Today the place is a Hallmark Card Shop.

'Give him a proper haircut this time,' my father had said.

'Sure enough, Mr Calhoun.'

Lloyd first snipped away the bangs with his scissors, and

then ran the electric clippers up the back and sides. Rankin closed his eyes, unable to bear the sight in the mirror.

My father watched over his newspaper.

'Can't you take a bit more off the top?'

Lloyd chuckled nervously.

'I don't know, Mr Calhoun. It's pretty short now. This boy going out for football?'

'Not if he had the choice,' said my father.

So Lloyd just smiled and ran his clippers up and over Rankin's scalp. My brother walked out of Steimel's that morning looking like Buzz Aldrin, mortified at the thought of school on Monday.

Driving home later after lunch, my father seemed to feel a pang of remorse.

'Looks like Lloyd got a little scissor-happy this time,' he said, smiling across at Rankin who stared in quiet misery out the passenger window.

'It'll grow back. Won't it now?'

'Yes sir,' Rankin mumbled.

'Of course it will.'

Sweetgum field – in the end – had little effect on the amount of time my father spent with us at home. He was soon back working long hours on another prospect. But it did bring about one major change in our family. The first we heard of it was one evening in late January, a few months after Sweetgum came on line. My father arrived home early from work with a cardboard map tube tucked under one arm. He made Ophelia clear away our dinner and then pulled out a large Tobin map and spread it across the kitchen table. Near the center a small rectangular segment had been shaded with a blue pencil.

'By this Saturday that'll be ours,' he said.

George had that afternoon signed a purchase agreement on 65 acres of land with a small house and barn. It was located about an hour north of New Orleans across Lake Pontchartrain in St. Tammany Parish.

'Near the pleasant rural hamlet of Buck Falaya,' read the realtor's particulars.

My father had already given the property a name. It was scrawled in pencil on the map – 'Larkspur'. But over the years, we came to know the place simply as 'the farm'.

Just why he decided to invest his oil profit in this way has never been exactly clear to me. That night he explained how we'd spend our weekends and summers away from the city. How there was plenty to do – cleaning and painting, new fences and barn repairs, a vegetable garden.

'Get some dirt under you boys' fingernails,' he'd said.

But it was still an odd, almost frivolous purchase for such a hard-minded businessman. My father never recouped half the money he sunk into the place – not to mention the sweat. But I think he had other reasons of his own for buying the property at Buck Falaya.

George Calhoun – as I said before – grew up on a small plantation that had been in his family for well over a century. I know the place only from photographs: a white clapboard house, with two storeys and an attic my Aunt Beth claims was roomy enough for a barn dance if her parents hadn't been such strict Baptists. A large front portico with six plain white columns gave the place a slightly formal air – though nothing imposing.

An ancestor named William J. Calhoun built the house in 1847, on two thousand acres of land he'd acquired through a land grant from the U.S. Government. He grew cotton and was a slave owner, and – before dying in the 1860s – raised four sons. He was buried next to his wife in a family cemetery in the middle of a cornfield behind the house. A succession of Calhouns subdivided and farmed the land over the generations, producing enough progeny to populate most of nearby Catalpa. Aunt Beth has a yellowed photograph of a 1935 reunion with the large front porch of the house almost sagging under the weight of accumulated Calhouns.

It was in the early 1920s when Frank Calhoun – our grandfather – negotiated with the rest of the family to buy the house and a hundred or so acres of surrounding land. No one had been living there for twenty years and the place was getting run down. He put on a new roof, wired in electricity, installed inside toilets and running water. He then moved in with his wife and Aunt Beth, who was just a baby. George was born in the house, as was my Aunt Lilian.

Frank Calhoun died years before Rankin and I were born. Aunt Beth has a photograph of him in her bedroom in Alexandria, a stern-looking man, though not unhandsome, tall and slim in a white linen suit. His hat is off and it's hard to tell if he's smiling or just squinting in the sunlight.

My grandmother lived alone in the house for another ten years after her husband's death. Nothing could induce her to move to a smaller place. Then in 1958 she suffered a severe stroke. A maid discovered her lying unconscious in a rose bed behind the house. From that day on she was bedridden. Aunt Beth arranged a place for her in a nursing home near Alexandria.

'It just killed your grandmother to leave that house,' Aunt Beth once told us, dabbing a dutiful tear from the corner of her eye.

'But there was no one to look after her up there, except maybe Lilian. And she just couldn't drag herself away from the bright lights.'

My Aunt Lilian was an unmarried art teacher in Chicago. Beth held her in suspicion on all counts.

The nursing home proved expensive. Soon my father and his sisters found they couldn't keep up with the payments. Aunt Beth and her husband John had five children to support.

So one weekend they all met up at the house and decided

it would have to be sold along with the land. A local man bought the property and used it to graze cattle. The house remained empty, at least until 1960 when some tramps broke in and set the place on fire – or perhaps the new owner did it himself. In any case, the house burnt to the ground.

My grandmother never even knew the place was sold, much less destroyed. She died a year later none the wiser.

Most of this we heard second-hand from Aunt Beth. Our father rarely spoke about the house, and never about the fire. Maybe it was just too upsetting – part of his childhood wiped away, the silent censure of my grandfather and all those other Calhouns crumbling away up in that graveyard abandoned among the corn rows. But I'm sure he had all this in the back of his mind when he signed that purchase agreement for the property at Buck Falaya.

A few years have passed since I last visited our farm. Yet I can still recall almost every detail of the trip up from New Orleans. The Buck Falaya turn-off is on the main Folsom highway north of the much larger town of Covington. It tends to sneak up on you. The sign is overgrown with jasmine and kudzu, and blasted through with buckshot. Most people miss the sign and end up turning around at the gravel entrance to Seven Oaks Quail Farm a quarter mile up the road.

Buck Falaya lies about six miles from the highway on LA 917, a battered asphalt road, warped and latticed with tar. It cuts through a thick pine forest owned mostly by The Chappapela Lumber Company. A few small farms lie off the road in long narrow strips bare of trees apart from live oaks to shade the houses and barns. The owner's names – Reed, Baham, Warner, Ellis – are painted in bright colors on huge, breadloaf mail boxes anchored in deep plugs of cement.

No sign announces Buck Falaya proper. The farms and houses just seem to get closer together, the mail boxes more numerous. Eventually you come to a sharp bend and cross the Bogue Falaya river on a groaning timber bridge that stinks of creosote. To the left is Marslan's Grocery, a small building with a flat tarred roof and peeling blue paint. A sagging wooden awning extends from the front over a concrete gas island with two ancient and disused Texaco pumps.

Across the highway is the Liberty Baptist Church. Next to that, set back from the road in a grove of cedar trees, is a large white wooden house with a broad porch enclosing it on three sides like a steamboat gallery. A sign on the front gate reads 'The Retreat', though the place is known locally as Pechon's Landing. The grounds are well tended, the grass always cut, and yet I can't say for certain if I've ever seen a Pechon.

A few more small houses lie out of town, along the road to Blond. But this is Buck Falaya for the most part. Passing through you might think it hardly worth a name at all. But the town is mentioned in local history books. General Andrew Jackson even passed nearby on his way south to organize the defense of New Orleans against the British in 1814. The General's engineer, Major H. Tatum, mentions it in his diary:

'Passed the old cantonment on Little Feliah (or little Long Creek) at 11 miles. Near this place there is an excellent Saw-Mill (at the settlement of Buck Falia). Proceeded in all 16½ miles to the Town of Wharton on the Bogue Feliah River (or Big Long Creek) a fork of the Chefonta River. The Indians call both these creeks Bogue Feliah, and distinguish them by the Greater & Smaller, or Big & Little, and these names are retained by the settlers.'

Tatum's rather garbled account of the geography sounds more like one a local dignitary might have fumbled for over a glass of bourbon. But Buck Falaya (cf Falia or Feliah) is cited again in later records as the location of a large saw mill operated as early as 1843 by a Lewis Pechon. The mill was driven by the clear, swift current of the Bogue Falaya –

the cut timber floated downstream to Covington on narrow flatboats. No apparent trace is left of the mill, but it must have been a success considering the fine architecture of Pechon's Landing.

Our farm lies a half mile or so beyond the town on a dusty gravel track off the main road. The track runs through a copse of young pines and eventually crosses a cattle guard. It then swings along the edge of a pasture and through a grove of oak trees, ending next to a wooden farmhouse with a steep, rust-streaked tin roof overhanging the front porch in the Creole-style. Out back is a vegetable garden, chicken coop, a brick-lined well and a small Dutch barn of old, seasoned timber. Little has changed about the place since my father first saw it that winter in 1965.

Driving back up the track towards town you pass another house on the right, a few hundred yards beyond the cattle guard. This one is now derelict – the clapboard brown and rotting, the tin roof peeled open by the wind. Weeds and briars choke the yard and sprout through the front porch. An old tractor pokes out the door of a collapsed farm shed, its flattened tires angled towards the gate as though it had died trying to escape the ruin. A well-aimed shotgun blast has bent the mail box back from its post and torn the lid half off. But the name is still barely legible in chipped red paint:

G. Reives

Chapter 3

My father drove us up to Buck Falaya for the first time that following Saturday. It was a cold, rainy afternoon. Ophelia and I sat drowsing in the back seat of the Oldsmobile with the warmth from the heater and the soft whine of the tires on the Lake Pontchartrain Causeway. Rankin sat in the front with my father, who was unusually talkative that day, setting out his plans for the farm.

Behind the house he would plant potatoes, and a few acres of corn out beyond the barn. Eventually he would buy a dozen head of cattle to graze in the large pasture. But fencing was his big worry. Most of the posts were rotten and he would have to order bails of new wire. Each time my father spoke of the farm his accent would undergo a sort of northward migration, from New Orleans through Baton Rouge to Alexandria, clear up to Ruston where folks put two syllables into words like 'talk' and 'damn'. It's hard to imagine this was completely unconscious.

A steady drizzle was falling by the time we reached the farm. Mud and gravel from the track clattered against the fenders as we drove into the yard. I remember the house looking gloomy under that dull sky, in the shadow of those sodden oaks. My first thought was that it must surely be haunted.

My father pulled the car up to the side of the house. Throwing a jacket over his head he dashed onto the porch and unlocked the front door. The wood was so swollen with damp that he had to put his shoulder to it to get inside. Ophelia then gathered us under an umbrella and we waded through the flooded grass up to the porch.

We found my father standing in the large front room. Daylight glowed faintly through dirty bedsheets which had been tacked over the windows. Other than a battered brown sofa overturned in the middle of the floor, the room was empty of furniture. Old newspapers and clothing were strewn over the bare cypress boards. The walls were covered in a yellowed floral paper, stained with damp in one corner. A brick fireplace with a tall pine mantle was built into the far wall, the grate choked with ash and half-burned letters and bills. A sweet, stale odour hung in the air, as though the place hadn't been opened in years.

Ophelia reached over to a window and tore away one of the bedsheets, which fell to the floor in a plume of dust.

'Lord above,' she said, and turned to survey the room in the better light.

'Nothing that a little elbow grease won't take care of,' said my father.

'Or a match,' she muttered.

But he only smiled and went out to unload the car.

Rankin and I wandered through the rest of the house. There was a short hall opening off the front room, with two small bedrooms and a bathroom containing an old cast iron tub. The kitchen was located at the rear of the house, its floor covered in worn, lime green linoleum. An ancient white enamelled gas range sat against one wall, along with a monstrous fridge/freezer, large enough to entrap and extinguish a half dozen neighborhood children at least.

Ophelia was already inspecting the cabinets and the deep stone sink. She turned one of the porcelain taps. Brown, rusty water sputtered into the drain and then gradually ran clear.

'None of your dirty river water here,' she said. 'This comes straight up from the ground. It's called an artesian well – you don't even need a pump.'

I had a sip from the spigot. The water was ice cold and tasted vaguely of boiled eggs.

Just out the kitchen door was a back porch enclosed with wire screening to keep out the mosquitoes. Ophelia called it a 'sleeping porch' and explained how people used to make their beds out there when the summer nights grew too hot.

By this time the rain was torrential, drifting in sheets across the yard. Each time the wind stirred the trees there was a deafening clatter on the tin roof. Rankin and I were given the task of gathering the trash off the floor into burlap sacks. Sifting through the rubbish we made a game of who could come up with the most interesting object. Ophelia placed the best ones on the mantlepiece.

Rankin managed to find an old Uniroyal Tire calender in one of the bedrooms. A faded brunette in a skimpy polkadot blouse leaned over the steering wheel of a red tractor, her lips pursed, blowing a kiss. The month was September 1954 – all the others had been torn away.

Among my discoveries was an iron horseshoe, an old technicolor postcard of Jackson Square, and a cracked teacup that read 'St Louis, Gateway to the West'. But Ophelia made the strangest find. Sweeping out the closet next to the fire she came upon an old-fashioned children's shoe – a tiny brown leather boot with tarnished brass buckles. There was something sad and vaguely menacing about it. I remember being afraid to look at that end of the mantlepiece.

A fire was now blazing in the hearth, and my father squatted beside it burning old newspapers. He wore a pair of stiff new blue jeans and a plaid flannel shirt and looked like some model Dad out of the Sears Catalogue. By then Rankin and I had filled nearly a dozen burlap sacks and stacked them at the front door. Ophelia made hot chocolate and we sat on a rug in front of the fire waiting for it to cool.

'Who lived here before?' I asked my father.

'Just an old farmer.'

'Mr Barton?'

I had seen this name on a number of old bills and junk mail envelopes.

'That's right.'

'Did he move?'

'Sort of.'

'Was it far away?'

'Not really,' he hedged.

'Then why did he leave all this stuff?'

'Because Mr Barton died, son.'

'Here?' Rankin asked.

My father turned to him in annoyance.

'Now how could that possibly matter. You boys finish your chocolate and take out that trash.'

So Rankin and I put on our raincoats and dragged the sacks, one by one, across the wet grass to the barn. Stowing the last just inside the door, Rankin said he wanted to have a look around.

The barn seemed an immense building to me then. Two rows of stalls lay along each side of a large central breezeway open to the ceiling and lit by a dirty skylight. The floor was covered in damp sawdust, and other than a few rusty tools, the place was empty.

A galleried hayloft lay above the stalls and across the

front of the building. Rankin soon found the ladder and hatch – up a wall in the tack room. He climbed the wooden rungs and disappeared through a square hole in the ceiling.

'Are there any rats up there?' I shouted.

'Hundreds,' he called back.

But on reaching the top of the ladder I found only a dusty wooden floor and a few crumbling hay bales. Rankin had unlatched the loading doors and swung them open. We sat with our feet dangling over the edge, looking out across the sodden brown pasture to the trees beyond. Here Rankin told me the true story behind the farm.

Mr Barton had not died at all but had, in fact, been locked up for the last ten years in Mandeville – the local insane asylum. My father had only been lying so as not to frighten us.

'Nobody knows why Old Bart went crazy,' said Rankin.

'A neighbor found him one day just sitting in his rocking chair, staring out into the woods. No one could get a word out of him. The ambulance finally came and took him away. He hasn't said anything for the last ten years. Not a word. But there were rumours.'

Rankin then told me how a number of boys had gone missing in the area over the years. First there was a boy-scout picking up litter down by the bridge.

'One minute he was going for his merit badge in citizenship,' said Rankin. 'The next minute – vanished. The police dragged the river. But all they pulled up was his Western Flyer.'

Next to disappear was the Folsom Junior High Spelling Bee champion – two years running. Then it was the Baptist minister's son. Three more boys vanished without a trace over the next few years.

'But the saddest of all,' said Rankin, 'was little Buddy Nelson. He was this sickly kid, small for his age. Disappeared one Halloween while out trick-or-treating. Later his mother went crazy: Buddy was her only child. Nobody knows what happened to him that night. Though one little girl thought she saw a tall bent figure in a heavy raincoat and farmer's hat hurrying away into the dark.'

Rankin glanced over at the house.

'They searched the area. The woods, the river, the fields. But all they ever found was this one little brown leather shoe with shiny buckles.'

'You're making it up,' I said.

'No. Dad told me not to say anything.'

'Liar!'

Rankin shrugged his shoulders.

'Why do you think we got the farm so cheap. Nobody else would live here.'

'I'm gonna ask Ophelia.'

I climbed down from the loft. Daylight was fading and the empty barn seemed darkly malevolent. I pushed open the doors and sprinted across the yard to the house. Climbing onto the kitchen porch I turned and looked back to the barn. Rankin was still sitting in the open loft doors, his grin lost in the shadows.

Ophelia had packed a light supper in the ice chest. Later that night we sat around the fire eating cold ham and potato salad off paper plates. Not long after the food was finished we heard the sound of heavy boots on the porch outside. Ophelia was clearing up in the kitchen and my father was packing his tools. There was a light knock at the door – little more than a tap.

'Now who's that?' said my father.

I looked over at Rankin. He raised his eyebrows in mock horror.

George struggled again with the door, but this time it wouldn't budge. Finally he called out: 'Could you give the door a shove please – it's swollen shut.'

A second later it swung open and banged against the wall. A man in a bulky green overcoat stood in the opening, his face lost in the shadow of a sodden straw hat.

For a moment I thought my heart had stopped. I glanced over at Rankin. Even he looked stricken. It was as though Old Bart had stepped right out his imagination like a tale from one of Claude's *Macabre* comic books.

The man leaned inside and ran his fingers along the edge of the door.

'Need to take a shave off that,' he said.

'There's a lot of things that need doing around here,' replied my father. 'So I take it you're a neighbor.'

'Yes sir. That's my house just over ya'll's cattle guard,' said the man. 'That is, I'm assuming this is your property. You don't look much like burglars to me.'

'No. We own the place – for better or worse.'

My father held out his hand.

'George Calhoun.'

'Pleased to meet you Mr Calhoun. The name's Gilbert Reives.'

The man then kicked his boots against the door jamb to shake off the mud before coming in. George took his wet coat and hung it on a nail by the fire.

'Not much of a night,' he said. 'Can I offer you a little something to cut the chill?'

Reives smiled for the first time.

'Butter in your hands Mr Calhoun.'

George disappeared into the kitchen. Reives sat on the edge of the sofa and nodded mutely at Rankin and me. He was at least fifteen years older than my father – a stocky man of medium height, with thin, receding dark hair. His face was broad and red. A purple lattice of broken capillaries ran across the skin of his nose and cheeks. His grey eyes looked glazed and slightly bloodshot.

A minute later my father returned with a bottle of Jack Daniels and two paper cups.

'Think this'll do the trick?'

'No question about it,' said Reives. 'Tell you if the temperature falls any more out there we might see some ice on the trees by morning.'

My father nodded gravely and poured two tall measures of whiskey into the cups. Reives bobbed his head in thanks and drained half his in one go.

'So rumour has it ya'll from New Orleans,' he said. 'Moving up here permanently?'

'No. I wish I could say so,' my father replied. 'It's just for weekends.'

'That's what I figured. Lots of folks from New Orleans getting weekend ranches up here. That's what they call 'em – ranches. Heard of one fella bought a twenty-acre tung nut grove up near Money Hill. Nothing more than an old shed on it and he calls it 'The Big Valley' – like the TV show.'

Reives laughed loudly. He then pulled out a pack of cigarettes and offered one to my father, who declined.

'So you got a name for this place?'.

'Thought we might call it Larkspur.'

'Larkspur, Larkspur – that some kind of bird?'

'No. It's a plant, actually. A flowering plant.'

'A flower? Never did learn my flowers,' said Reives, smiling into his cup.

'So what do you call your place?' My father asked.

'Hell, I suppose if I had to call my place anything, it'd be just Plain Trouble.'

Reives laughed loudly again. Ophelia then came in from the kitchen, and my father stood up to make introductions.

'This is Mr Reives, Ophelia. Our nearest neighbor.'

'Pleased to meet you,' she said.

Reives nodded but made no move to stand. He glanced up at George with an odd smile and then leaned back on the sofa and took another long look around the room.

'So what's your line of work Mr Calhoun?'

'Geologist – oil and gas. I used to work for a company in New Orleans. But now I'm independent.'

'Looks like you struck a big one.'

George smiled.

'We're doing okay.'

Reives winked at him and took another sip from his whiskey.

'Worked a while in the oil business myself,' he said. 'Roustabout out of Morgan City. Now that's a rough town. No place for a country boy.'

'So what do you do now?' asked my father.

'Oh I keep a few cows. No big operation mind you. Most of my time now I just spend doing things for folks.'

'You mean odd jobs?'

'You could call it that. Fixing cars, painting houses, carpentry. Got a tractor mower. Do some mowin'. What ever needs done. I also raise rabbits – though I'm just getting started with that.'

'Really? Is there much money in rabbits?'

'You'd be surprised,' said Reives.

'Restaurants, grocers, pet shops – especially around Easter time. I sell mostly to a wholesaler and he does pretty well. Told me that he once supplied four dozen rabbits to the college over at Wharton. Heard some scientist was clipping off their ears and putting them into a room with a barking dog. Don't ask me why.'

'That's horrible,' said Ophelia.

Reives looked over at her with a blank expression. There was an uncomfortable silence. My father then reached over and poured two more cups of whiskey.

'Well, it's good to meet someone from the neighborhood,' he said.

Reives regained his smile.

'Just glad to see the place lived in again. Been what . . . nearly four years since Barton died? Strange old fellow. I can't say we got on too well. Just wasn't very sociable. Lived here nearly twenty years on his own after his wife died. Had a daughter over in Texas.'

'A Mrs Stewart,' said my father. 'I had a letter from her before the act of sale. Said she was really sorry to let the place go.'

'Can't say why,' said Reives. 'She only visited once or twice a year, along with her kids. Little devils. Caught 'em once herding my chickens up towards the highway. Barton did next to nothing about it. But like I said we were never friendly.'

My father let this pass.

'So how is this area for break-ins, that sort of thing?'

'Not bad really,' said Reives. 'Every once in a while you get some motorcycle gang passing through. Broke into one weekend house over on Lee Road. Nobody saw 'em, but they made a hell of a mess. Poured beer all over the place.'

'You wouldn't think there'd be too many motorcycle gangs wandering around up here.'

'Oh yea. They come hunting them little mushrooms that grow in cow dung, you know. Boil them into tea. Supposed to get 'em high. Just the thought of it turns my stomach.'

My father grinned uncertainly.

'The reason for asking is that I'm just a little worried about leaving the place unattended. I'd like to find someone local to keep an eye on it. I'm also planning to make some improvements here and there. Maybe we could come to some arrangement. That is, if you're interested. Maybe you know somebody else?'

'Why I'd be glad to help out, Mr Calhoun.'

George poured out another two measures of whiskey to seal the agreement.

'So you done much farming before?' Reives asked.

'Not in quite a while. I was raised on a farm up in Lyndon Parish.'

'So now you want to get your hands back in the soil,'

said Reives, his head bobbing. 'Sometimes I feel that way. Fortunately not too often.'

He chuckled and stood up, abruptly.

'Listen, I better get on home now. Stop by the next time you're up. Meantime I'll keep an eye on the place. Don't you worry.'

'We'd sure appreciate that.'

Reives drained his cup, and my father walked him to the door. He then looked back over his shoulder at Rankin and me.

'Next time send your boys up to the house. They might like to see my rabbits. Sure my daughter'd have a couple pieces of pie squirreled away somewhere.'

With that he put on his coat and hat and disappeared out into the rain. My father closed the door and shook his head, smiling.

'That man's got some line.'

'Don't know if I like him much,' said Ophelia.

'Oh, he's harmless enough. Plenty like him back home where I grew up.'

Ophelia gathered up the half-empty whiskey bottle and muttered to herself:

'I just bet there are.'

Chapter 4

A week or so later the weather grew exceptionally cold for New Orleans. For five days the temperature barely rose above freezing. Palm trees along Carrollton Avenue began to brown with the frost. Banana plants and elephant ears wilted and drooped over garden walls and patios like deflated pool toys. Pipes burst all over the city, showering out from under the houses, turning the azalea bushes into glistening ice sculptures. Water pressure dropped to a trickle.

Then one morning a high grey cloud drifted over the city and it began to sleet. Fine grains of ice clattered over the cars and down the rain gutters – a sound I'd never heard before. The nuns at St Francis gave up trying to maintain order in the classrooms. No one could keep their eyes away from the windows and this small miracle for southern Louisiana. By noon the lights had started to flicker with ice gathering on the powerlines. Sister Joan d' Arc then announced on the intercom in the cafeteria that she was sending everyone home before the storm grew worse. A shrill cheer arose from the tables, so piercing that Sister Margaret had to cover her ears. Such a contingency was usually reserved only for hurricanes.

Ranks of school buses appeared outside the main building, their exhausts steaming in the cold. Ophelia was waiting for us in the station wagon, as she had heard the announcement on the radio. Rankin ran his hand across the windshield and scooped up a handful of sleet which he packed into a sloshy ball and sent sailing across the street at the window of a school bus.

But what I remember most is later that afternoon, standing in the backyard and looking up to see the first heavy wet flake, then another, until the sleet had given way to snow. Neither Rankin nor I had ever seen snow before. The clarity of the memory amazes me.

The wind carried the flakes with a quiet hiss, like the rustling of silk curtains. The sound of traffic, the cries of children, grew oddly muffled and blunt. At first the snow melted as it hit the ground, but slowly flakes began to gather on the wet grass and to cling absurdly to the waxy green leaves of the live oaks and magnolias.

It snowed most of the night, about two inches – breaking a sixty year record. The next morning I was woken by Rankin standing at the window.

'Come look,' he said. 'Everything's different now.'

The snow had stopped except for a few flurries carried on the wind from high wispy clouds. A thick white blanket covered the yard, the reflected light filling every shadow. Overnight our world had been transformed. Franklin Place seemed now a different street entirely, one somewhere in that nameless 'North' celebrated in every grade school reader I'd ever known.

Ophelia's radio blasted from the kitchen; an announcer was reading out a list of public and private school closures for the day. Hearing St Francis Xavier read out, Rankin danced around Ophelia, boxing at her arm.

'I'm sending you anyway,' she said. 'I'm sure Sister Joan'd look after you in her nice warm office.'

Outside the air was crisp and the sky an intense blue. Rankin was exuberant as we left the house after breakfast, pushing me into the snow, rubbing it into my face. The golf course at Orleans Country Club had been transformed into a vast snowy field. Dozens of kids had converged on it that morning – some I'd never seen before and never would again, black and white.

Snowball battles erupted. Boys sledded down the raised greens on flattened cardboard boxes. Girls fell back into the drifts and made 'snow angels' with their arms and legs, just as they'd read about in *Highlights Magazine*.

A freeze set in again after sunset, though less harsh than in previous nights. Next morning we awoke to find the snow melting. Steady rivulets of water streamed off the roof into the gutters and down the storm drains. Cool balmy air drifted up from the Gulf, too mild for a heavy coat yet too cold for a sweater alone – weather more typical of New Orleans in January. Franklin Place re-emerged looking even more brown and charmless than before.

That morning my father got a call at his office from Gilbert Reives. A pipe under the house at the farm had cracked with the frost and was now flooding the yard. Rieves had himself promised to wrap the pipes during the week, when the cold weather was first predicted. But he claimed to have been sick with the flu.

'Hit me like a freight train Mr Calhoun,' he said on the phone. 'Barely managed to get my own pipes wrapped.'

Then almost in the same breath he mentioned the name of a cousin in Blond who did plumbing work. Reives even helped him out on occasion. So my father arranged to meet the two that afternoon at the farm. He drove across the Lake straight from work, still in his business suit.

*

Rankin had refused to leave the house all that day. He lay in front of the TV in his sleeping bag. The change in weather had put him in a sullen mood.

'Who wants to stand around like a moron and watch snow melt,' he'd said when I suggested we go back to the golf course. So I went out into the yard alone, and kicked at the snow still lying in the shadows.

Later that afternoon I heard the Oldsmobile pull into the driveway. I ran to the gate and found my father lifting a cardboard box off the floor of the back seat.

'Go get your brother,' he said to me.

A dozen or so holes were punched in the top of the box, which was labelled 'Monroe Peaches'.

'Are those from Aunt Beth?' I asked, peering around the car door.

That's when the smell hit me: an acrid, eye-watering stench.

'What is that?'

'Never you mind,' my father snapped. 'Just go get your brother.'

So I ran into the house and shouted for Rankin. He shuffled, frowning, to the kitchen doorway in his socks. Then his jaw dropped in total disbelief. For my father had just then breezed through the gate, the box held at arm's length, a small white piglet leaning over the side, its pink ears and snout smeared in shit.

'Fill up the back sink with water,' he shouted.

'Where did you get it?' Rankin asked.

'Don't worry about that now son. Just fill up the sink.'

Rankin dashed across the yard into the utility room which adjoined our garage. My father followed him through the doorway and laid the box on the draining board. The piglet seemed unperturbed. Rankin shut off the tap when the basin was half full with warm water. My father then reached into the box and grabbed the piglet with both hands.

Nothing can even approximate the wrenching shriek

that animal let loose – like two sharpened pencils jammed through your eardrums. Rankin and I cupped our hands to our heads. My father's face grew pale with fury.

He just managed to maneuver the piglet out of the box and into the sink. It kicked and twisted, throwing half the water out onto the floor. Then it hooked its forehocks over the edge of the basin, eyes rolling back in panic. The shriek modulated to a sharp, rhythmic squeal. My father – for some odd reason – decided that the water must be too hot. So he grabbed the animal again by its forehocks and lifted it up out of the basin. That's when the piglet began to crap.

For a moment George just stood there aghast – brown runny turds plopping onto the floor, splattering his shoes. Finally he threw it back into the sink.

'Hold on till I find another box.'

Neither of us dared look him in the face. His white shirt and tie were drenched, his sleeves smeared with brown excrement. Outside the door, he slipped off his dirty shoes and socks and walked back to the house barefoot.

Rankin stood by the basin and held out his hand to keep the piglet from scrambling over the side.

'Nowhere for you to go anyway.'

He then grinned to himself.

'Bombs away. Right on his shoe.'

'Better not let Dad hear you,' I said.

But Rankin just ignored this. He soaped his hands and calmly began to wash the animal, speaking to it in an odd, soothing voice, like a cooing Elmer Fudd.

'Settle down there, mister pig.'

I started to laugh.

'Shut it, Milo.'

The piglet squirmed through my brother's hands. But the squealing had stopped and the animal seemed less panicked. Soon my father returned from the house. Instead of a box, he brought out an old wooden play pen which had been used to coral Rankin as a toddler. He unfolded it in the garage and lined the bottom with a layer of newspapers.

Rankin carried the wet pig out to the pen. We then stood and watched it bumping its snout along the wooden bars, looking for an escape.

'Not very smart,' I said.

But Rankin wasn't listening. He crouched down next to the pen and pressed the back of his hand against the bars. Eventually the pig stopped pacing and snuffled at his fingers. My father opened the garage door and unloaded four large sacks of pig feed from the trunk of the car. He also grabbed a brown paper parcel off the front seat and handed it to my brother.

'We're only keeping it until it's big enough to go up to the farm,' he said.

Rankin opened the parcel. Inside was a battered hardback book, the jacket faded as though it had sat for years in a shop window. It was entitled *A Hog Farmer's Companion*, by the Hon. Edmund J. Taylor.

'The breeder recommended it,' said my father. 'Told me you'll find everything you need to know, and a lot more that you don't.'

'Think you can handle this?' He then asked.

Rankin nodded.

'Now this isn't a pet; it's a farm animal. You understand me.'

'Yes sir.'

'Fine then. Let your brother help some.'

George went back into the house to change. A few minutes later Ophelia arrived home from the grocery store, pulling up to the garage in the station wagon. She climbed out the car and called:

'Is that what I think it is?'.

'A pig,' I shouted.

'Lord, Lord. What's your Daddy up to now?'

'It's for the farm.'

Ophelia shook her head and strolled into the garage, peering over the edge of the playpen.

'Sure not the pick of the litter.'

'What's the matter with it?' asked Rankin.

'Just looks kind of puny. Think somebody done sold your Daddy the runt.'

'What do you know about pigs?'

'A lot more than you do, boy,' said Ophelia. 'See how his ribs are showing, and the tail just sort of hanging. Healthy pig got a little curl to its tail.'

'Will it die?'

'Ain't nothing gonna die. Just needs some fatten up.'

Ophelia then carried in her groceries, and later came back out to the garage with a baking dish of diluted milk. Rankin laid the dish inside the pen and the piglet quickly vacuumed it dry.

'Got a healthy appetite, at least,' said Ophelia. 'Give it a week or two of good feeding and it'll be alright.'

Then she lowered her voice.

'Your Daddy really gonna keep this thing here?'

'For now,' said Rankin.

'Lordy me.'

'So how do you know so much about pigs?'

Ophelia crouched next to the play pen.

'My Uncle Clifton used to keep pigs. I even raised one myself for 4-H. Wasn't much older than you at the time.'

'You raised a pig?'

'Yes sir. Uncle Cilfton gave me the pick of litter from one of his sows. You can always tell which is the healthiest 'cause they the ones that suckle at the head end. I called him Lil' Abner, after the cartoon. Raised him from about six weeks. I had to keep a record of how much he weighed, how much food he ate. I made a chart and wrote it down each week.'

'How big did he get?'

'Just before I took Abner to the 4-H Fair he weighed about four hundred pounds.'

'Pigs get that big?'

'Oh they get a lot bigger than that. But Abner was heavy for his age. Took a lot of feeding. He was sneaky too. Learned how to slip the rope off his gate and get into the trash. Not that we had much food left to throw out with him around.'

'So did he win at the fair?'

'No,' she said. 'Still makes me mad to think about it. I remember that day Uncle Clifton took us to the fairgrounds in his truck. We had to unload Abner into this little pen in the livestock barn – so small he couldn't even turn around. I spent all day waiting by that pen for the judges. First two come along. They white men, of course. Both of them smiling at me like they about to die laughing. Big colored girl and her pig. They walk around the pen and one of them asks, 'What you been feeding this pig, girl?' So I hold up my chart. But the other one just says 'A *mess* a' chitlins.' Both of them burst out laughing and just go on to the next pen. Didn't even ask any questions.'

'Later on this white lady came along with a clipboard. She was a lot nicer, and asked me how I set my project up. Let me explain my chart and how I fed him from mainly kitchen slop so that it cost next to nothing. She told me it was an excellent project. So I thought sure I'd win.'

'So why didn't you?'

''Cause they end up giving the blue ribbon to some buck tooth white girl from New Roads who hatched a few quail eggs in her daddy's incubator. Uncle Clifton was so mad. He took Abner home and slaughtered him that night. Had to give the bacon away. My momma and I just didn't have the heart to eat it.'

'I don't believe that,' said Rankin.

'Better believe it boy.'

Though I don't think it was the injustice of Ophelia losing that bothered Rankin so much as the thought that anyone could even contemplate eating a creature named Abner.

Just before bedtime that night Rankin brought an electric heater out to the garage and arranged a couple of burlap sacks in a corner of the pen. Ophelia filled a hot water bottle and tucked it underneath the sacks.

Later that night, long after bedtime I heard Rankin sneak into the room. He slipped off his shoes and jeans and climbed into bed still in his underwear.

'Did Ophelia know you were out there?' I whispered.

'No,' he said, turning his head away from me on the pillow.

'Was it asleep?'

'Put a sock in it, Milo.'

'Was it?'

'Like a baby.'

Over the next few weeks the weather remained humid and mild and the piglet spent most of its time out in the yard, mostly in motion. Just as Ophelia predicted, the regular feeding quickly transformed the animal. Each day it seemed to grow more plump and cigar shaped. Its hams grew muscular and its coat took on a satiny sheen. An absurd-looking kink developed in its tail.

At first the piglet hated being handled in any way. It would squeal and squirm in your hands, desperate to struggle free. Rankin was afraid to even open the pen in case it escaped and we couldn't catch it again. But after a week or two of gentle words and coaxing with treats like apples or mashed bananas, the piglet began to follow us around the yard like a puppy.

Weeks passed before Rankin got around to giving the pig a name. I constantly pestered him with suggestions.

'How about Porky?'

'Very original.'

'Arnold?'

'Taken.'

'Charlotte?'

'You mean Wilbur, dumbshit. Charlotte was the spider.'

'Then Wilbur?'

'Go play in traffic, Milo.'

But eventually Rankin did settle on a name. The idea came from the book the pig breeder had recommended to my father. Rankin had read most of *A Hog Farmer's Companion* within a few days. As farm books go, this must be one of the oddest ever written.

The author, Judge Edmund J. Taylor, was born a planter's son in Bonner, Mississippi 'ten years after the Civil War'. So reads the jacket blurb, just below a photo of an elderly man, broad and heavy jowled with silver hair and a grey suit.

Little else is noted except that Judge Taylor earned a B.A. in pedagogy from the University of Virginia and a law Degree from Ole Miss, and that he presided over the 8th District Court of Mississippi for over a quarter of a century, 'upholding the fine laws of that state'. This, I imagine, involved sending armed robbers and rapists to the Jackson Penitentiary, and murderers to a leather-braced electric chair up in Pinkneville. All in addition to keeping niggers clear of the bright chrome fonts of white-only water fountains throughout his district.

The blurb ends:

'On retiring from the courts to his family home in Bonner, Judge Taylor enjoyed the time and leisure to complete a project close to his heart: a simple text on the care and breeding of swine'.

But *A Hog Farmer's Companion* is more than just a manual of husbandry. Certainly it covers all aspects of hog care – from birth to butcher. Nothing is missed out. Yet it's also written with a curious passion, a reformist zeal.

'To elevate the pig from the mire of prejudice and contumely' as the Judge explains without a touch of irony in his preface.

'No animal on God's great Earth has suffered such depths of derision as has *Sus scrofa*. Man has long seen fit, for some unconscionable reason, to project the worst of his nature onto this most undeserving creature. How often do we hear that a man 'eats like a hog' or 'sweats like a pig.' And yet most hogs are, in fact, quite discriminating eaters, and pigs, as any southern keeper knows, haven't a great capacity to sweat. This is why they like to wallow in the summertime, to keep their brains from boiling . . . As for intelligence, few animals can boast an intellect superior to that of the pig – not the brightest spaniel nor the most sure-footed thoroughbred.'

To further prove his point the Judge cites Virgil, Horace, Shakespeare, Whitman, Victor Hugo – just about any writer who's ever mentioned a pig. Historical references, meanderings into theology and moral philosophy, ruminations on the nature of the soul – all this woven into a quite practical farming book. On one page the Judge might be feeding a three foot enema hose through the tail end of a sow; on the next he's reliving the boar hunt in Ossian or quoting from the English critic C.K. Chesterton: 'The actual lines of a pig (I mean of a really fat pig), are among the loveliest and most luxuriant in nature; the pig has the same great curves, swift and yet heavy, which we see in rushing water or in a rolling cloud.'

Judge Taylor apparently kept quite a large number of hogs on his own plantation in Bonner, many of which appear in the book under the names of past Republican presidents. In the chapter on Swine Disease, for example, he writes:

One crisp winter's morning William Howard Taft (a 400 lb boar) appeared at the trough with all the classic symptoms of swine dysentry, which is not to be confused with infectious diarrhoea, a more common affliction. Morning feed was taken with the usual relish, but his rear haunches bore the sad traces of a most uncomfortable evening, soiled as they were with a mixture of dung, blood and mucus. Plenty of fresh water and regular monitoring of the dunging area were on order and the infection soon cleared without need for the veterinary surgeon . . . .

But the pride of Judge Taylor's stock was a half ton Duroc boar – winner of two blue ribbons at the 1937 Mississippi State Agricultural Show. A photograph of this giant pig can be found on the frontispiece of *A Hog Farmer's Companion*. Rankin was so taken with the picture he tore out the page and tacked it above his desk. I can still remember the caption – word for word:

Traveller
Named in honor of General Lee's famous grey warhorse, the noblest creature ever to serve a man.

Chapter 5

I have a photograph taken by my grandfather one spring afternoon in 1965. Rankin is standing next to Traveller out in the backyard of the house on Franklin Place, while I ride on the pig's back, my school shoes barely touching the grass. A mild smile breaks across my face – the same one I seem to wear in almost every childhood photograph. Yet Rankin looks oddly sombre, his arms folded, eyes stern like a young soldier's in an antique daguerreotype. Only the pig seems to be truly at ease, his snout raised as though in smiling approval.

My grandfather had come over that afternoon for no other reason than to take this photograph. I can imagine him sniggering as he framed the shot, one eye pinched shut, his hand reaching around the front of the tripod to focus the Konika camera, an unfiltered cigarette dangling out of his mouth.

'Just look natural, boys,' he might have said to us at that

moment, coughing out jets of smoke.

By then Big Dad was already in his seventies, a pale, unhealthy looking man with narrow shoulders which he held always in a languid slouch that made his arms look long and puppet-like. He wore a light straw hat in rain or shine and baggy pleated trousers pulled almost to his chest and held there by suspenders. He spoke with a deep, gravelly murmur – a 'gin and midnight' voice.

For years Big Dad kept that photograph tucked in the frame of an old oil painting of mallard ducks taking flight from a flooded marsh. The print hung above a large rolltop mahogany desk in his 'studio' – actually a chaotic workshop which had originally been built as slave quarters for the house on Prytania.

Here Big Dad lived like a lodger in his own house, repairing odd bits of furniture, reading the *States Item* and the *Wall Street Journal*, painting watercolors of game birds modeled from photos in the *Louisiana Sportsman*. Other than the desk, a wooden workbench and some shelves, the only other furniture in the room was a small iron infirmary bed on which Big Dad took his naps. Above it hung a wooden crucifix with an ancient Lenten palm frond tucked behind it. On the bedside table was a photograph frame with a black and white portrait of my mother taken at the time of her high school graduation.

The studio was always thick with cigarette smoke. Despite his ill health Big Dad went through at least two packs of Lucky Strike per day. A lit cigarette hung perpetually from his lips, burning like a slow fuse until the ash grew long and bent, and then dropped unheeded into his lap. On the days Molly didn't clean in the studio, heaps of yellowed butts would accumulate in the corroded jar lids he used for ashtrays. Over the years the wallpaper had taken on a sallow brownish hue, such that when Big Dad's crucifix was removed after his death, the pattern remained branded on the wall like a photographic exposure.

Big Mum never set foot in the studio (which she called 'the atelier'). Not that this bothered Big Dad – it was probably the prime attraction. Neither seemed to really like the other much.

Big Dad rarely spoke of our mother. Maybe he found it just too painful. But I do remember him once pointing to that studio portrait on his bedside table.

'Now your mother was no saint,' he said. 'No matter what your Big Mum would have you think. But she was a pleasure to be around, full of life and humor, not a bitter, unhappy person by nature. So don't you boys ever believe otherwise.'

Neither Rankin nor I knew quite what he meant by this but we both nodded solemnly.

My only other enduring memory of my grandfather is riding in his big blue Chrysler LeBaron through some of the poorest black neighborhoods in Uptown New Orleans. No matter what his destination Big Dad always seemed to have a short-cut down one of these streets. It was as though he sought them out. He would cruise past the crumbling Victorian houses and red brick projects, heedless of the angry stares, the shouts from groups of young men lounging on the sidewalk. New Orleans in those years was near boiling point. The evening news broadcast almost nightly reports of racial incidents and civil rights demonstrations in other Southern cities.

Big Dad never watched these reports. He would quietly switch channels, or turn off the TV set. Never once did I hear him use the word nigger, or express a single racist sentiment in my presence. He was nothing less than polite to Molly. But in driving down those streets in that expensive, air-conditioned cocoon he seemed to be making some perverse statement. I grew up with the certainty that one day he'd die in a hail of bricks, pulled from the LeBaron at the center of an angry mob. In the end he had a heart attack while in the bathroom shaving.

Big Mum cleared out the studio, and gave us the photograph of Traveller along with a number of other momentos. Among them a gold Hamilton watch awarded to Big Dad in 1949 when he retired from his law firm, and the Konika camera with its complicated Swiss light meter which neither Rankin nor I have ever managed to operate.

It must have been early May, the afternoon Big Dad set up his tripod on the patio while Rankin coaxed the pig to stand still for those few moments. School had not yet finished. Both Rankin and I are still wearing our khaki uniforms. Traveller must not have been more than six or seven months old, but he had grown at an amazing rate. No more a skittish runt – it was a proper market hog now living in our backyard in the heart of Old Metairie.

Just how my father allowed this situation to develop is still beyond my complete understanding. But such was his tendency to invent a reality if that before his eyes proved too onerous or emotive. I used to think this was arrogance, but now I realise it was just my father's way of keeping life manageable, under control. Even when George took definite notice of Traveller's size, one day watching the pig root at the back edge of our fence, it was a much smaller animal he saw, probably no more offensive than Mrs. Pierrepont's cocker spaniel Shotzy. Rankin had – that same day – calculated Traveller's weight at 200 pounds. But my father flat didn't believe it.

'Son, you just haven't been around hogs as much as I have,' he said.

But the situation had not escaped the notice of our neighbors. Keeping Traveller had at first seemed only mildly eccentric – if not charming – to the residents of Franklin Place. They began to call us the 'pig people'. But the first hint of real annoyance came one morning a few weeks before St. Francis

Xavier let out for summer.

The days were already muggy and hot. Sitting in a class-room had become unbearable – especially in the afternoons. Everything had a somnolent feel: the sweep of the second hand on the electric wall clock above the blackboard, the drone of Sister Mary Martin on the formation of the Axis Powers, the soft white noise of the rotating fans at the front of the classroom. To fight the urge to sleep I would press a pen cap deep into the palm of my hand until the pain cleared my head.

Mid-afternoon, seeing there was no sense in fighting it, Sister would usually let us lay our heads down for ten minutes while she went to splash water on her face at the fountain in the hallway. Resting my forehead on the desk I'd bury my nose deep into the spine of *Our American Heritage*. There was a particular smell, the effect of the heat and humidity on the glue in the binding, a sweet, pulpy odour. To me this was the smell of summer and freedom.

That particular morning I was awake at exactly six a.m. – as I had been every morning since January. For the first few weeks Rankin had relied on an old alarm clock to get him out of bed to feed Traveller. But I so dreaded the sudden clatter in the dark that I began to wake up in anticipation, checking the luminous dial on my watch. A minute before six I would shout to Rankin to turn off the alarm. So after a while he no longer bothered to even set it.

Heedless of me, Rankin switched on all the lights and slipped into his jeans and a T-shirt. I lay in bed drowzing as he tied his sneakers and then disappeared downstairs without a word. Soon I heard the groan of the pipes in the kitchen as he began to fill a bucket with hot water.

Outside Traveller waited at the back stoop. I could hear him through the open window pressing against the screen door below. A few minutes later Rankin unlocked the kitchen door, and the pig pushed forward with low throaty grunts of excitement.

'Move,' Rankin whispered.

He then made his way across the yard into the garage, carrying the steaming bucket. Traveller followed at his heel. A second later he re-emerged pushing a wheelbarrow. A shovel rattled in the bed, and the bucket now swung from one of the handles. The wheelbarrow squeaked over the grass to a far corner of the yard. Here along the back edge of Mrs Pierrepont's fence and the Conroy's next door was Traveller's 'dunging area' – in Judge Taylor parlance. It was a broad patch of churned-up earth, a mud hole when it rained. A sickly mimosa tree grew nearby, bare of leaves, its outer branches already showing signs of rot.

Rankin made constant battle against this plot of ground. Each morning he would scrape up the muck with a shovel, and then pour a solution of hot water, ammonia and bleach over the spot in an attempt to keep the smell down. This worked somewhat while temperatures stayed mild, but as the days grew warm and humid an unmistakable stench began to drift over the neighborhood.

That morning Rankin sent up a cloud of flies as he shoveled the muck into the wheelbarrow. Traveller circled the spot in agitation, turning the soil with his snout, biting at the flies that swarmed about his head. Rankin then pushed the half-filled barrow back to the side of the garage, and opened the door to the utility room toilet. Shovel by shovel he then flushed it away – an immensely practical solution to my mind. But by then volumes had grown so large the whole process took nearly half an hour.

The morning was already hot and airless, and the stink grew so intense I had to close my window. I got up and dressed, and went downstairs for breakfast. Rankin was already at the sink mixing up pig feed – measuring out portions which he then recorded in a spiral notebook tied on a piece of string to the side of the cabinet. Ophelia leaned over her coffee mug on the breakfast table, unusually quiet. Traveller pressed his snout against the screen door, watching Rankin's every move.

An old white enamelled iron sink out in the yard served as the pig trough. Rankin had dragged it out from the breezeway under the house. For Traveller this sink was an object of great desire. Not an hour went by when he didn't check to see if it was still empty.

There was no hint of false dignity or restraint in Traveller's eating habits. Even as the slop bucket was being tipped into the trough he would nip at the edge, urging it on. Then as the milky feed spilled out he would thrust his snout under the stream, splattering it across his face and down the side of his mouth. He ate with a desperate urgency, in constant motion, his rump moving about the sink like the second hand of some kitsch wrist watch. Finishing, he would then clean the entire surface until the enamel gleamed, and reconnoitre the surrounding grass for any stray drips. Nothing was missed.

That morning Ophelia called Rankin inside to eat his breakfast. My father had offered to drive us to school and Rankin was already running late. But instead of making her usual start at the breakfast dishes, Ophelia sat in the chair opposite my brother as he spooned down his cereal.

'We gonna have to do something about that yard,' she whispered.

Rankin looked up.

'What's the matter with it?'

'Come on now. I can even smell it with the door closed.'

'I don't smell anything.'

'That's just cause you had your nose in it all morning. Do you think the neighbors gonna put up with that stink much longer?'

'Mrs. Pierrepont hasn't said anything.'

'Mrs. Pierrepont can't smell any better than she can hear,' said Ophelia. 'Anyhow I'm gonna have to have a word with your Daddy.'

'Ah come on Ophelia,' Rankin moaned.

'Honey, that pig don't belong out there. It might have been okay for a few months – but not now that he's so big. Time your Daddy brought him up to the farm.'

Rankin stared down into his breakfast.

'. . . or maybe not to the farm.'

'What's that supposed to mean?' Ophelia replied.

But Rankin didn't answer. Just then my father called from the den to say he'd wait for us out in the car. Rankin went upstairs to change. I gathered my books and walked out to the driveway. George had settled behind the steering wheel with his newspaper. I climbed into the backseat, and he glanced up into the rearview mirror.

'Read your school books,' he said.

But then something else caught his eye. I turned around to find Mr. Conroy from next door walking up the drive. My father got out of the car and strolled back to meet him halfway. Conroy was a civil engineer, a tall man with a rather doleful face that reminded me a little of Fred McMurray.

He and my father shook hands and began to walk slowly back toward the street. Conroy seemed to do most of the talking. My father occasionally jerked his head in agreement, and then reaching the street he began to kick lightly at the St. Augustine grass that had grown over the edge of the sidewalk. Conroy in his dark suit towered over him like a grade school principal. Then there was another brisk handshake and my father marched quickly back up the drive. I could tell he was furious.

Climbing back into the car he slammed the door and blasted the horn for Rankin. Ophelia appeared on the front porch and began waving her hand in annoyance. Rankin dashed out from behind her in his bare feet, shoes and socks stacked on top of the books under his arm, his shirt tail still untucked.

'This just isn't good enough,' my father muttered as Rankin climbed into the passenger seat.

Nothing more was said until we were out on Metarie Road heading toward school.

'So how are things going with the pig?' my father asked.

'Okay,' Rankin replied.

'Have you been cleaning up after him?'

'Yes sir.'

'You telling me the truth?'

'Yes sir.'

'Well, Mr. Conroy just had a word with me. He says the smell from our yard is just about peeling the paint off his house. He says that Mrs. Conroy nearly succumbs everytime she steps out onto her deck.'

Rankin made no reply.

'He also promised to inform the Health Department unless we do something about it. Now I'm gonna get in touch with Mr Reives today and arrange to have something done about that pig. But in the meantime I want you to clean up that backyard properly. Is that understood?'

Rankin nodded.

We reached St Francis. Rankin and I got out of the car in front of the main building. George then leaned through his open window.

'Don't let me have to tell you again,' he said and then pulled away.

Rankin and I walked through the gate into the main schoolyard. The first bell had rung and my class was already marching into home room. I hesitated a moment.

'You clean that yard every morning. I watch you.'

But Rankin only shrugged his shoulders and set off in a jog across the playground to the Junior High Building.

My father did telephone Buck Falaya that day but Reives was full of excuses – his truck needed a new clutch, the axle on the trailer had a crack, his sciatica was acting up. He promised to come up that Saturday. But the weekend passed with no sign of him. Mr Conroy again threatened to phone the Health Department and my father assured him the pig would be gone that week. But it wasn't until an incident a few days later that George became insistent with Reives.

Rankin blamed me entirely for what happened with Traveller that afternoon, and I suppose he was justified. Certainly he and I had very different ideas when it came to the pig.

Rankin's attitude to Traveller – on the face of it – was oddly impassive. Not that he was ever neglectful. Caring for Traveller was almost an obsession. To this end he pored over *A Hog Farmer's Companion*, taking Judge Taylor's lead in everything – even down to the degree of affection he showed.

'Kind words and an occasional scratch on the back: any more is unhelpful.'

Perhaps this was just my brother's way of steeling himself against what he saw as inevitable. But for whatever reason Rankin found my attitude towards the pig infuriating.

To me Traveller was a marvel from the very first moment he landed in that sink of hot water in our utility room. I had never seen anything so animate in my life, possessive of the sheer audacity to crap on my father's shoe. I was captivated.

I remember the first time Rankin let Traveller loose in the backyard. The piglet bolted across the grass and was impossible to catch, dodging and feinting with amazing instinct. Only by enticing him onto the patio with a bowl of milk was Rankin able to catch hold of his back legs and lift him squealing into the wooden pen. I reached down to lay my hand lightly on the piglet's rough coat only to have him swing around and bite me hard on the thumb.

But as Traveller quickly lost his fear of the new surroundings he became an inexhaustable playmate. Each day after school I spent hours chasing him around the yard, throwing tennis balls and shoes which he learned to fetch as well as any retriever. Using grapes as rewards I trained him to sit on command and to stay. Even after he'd grown into a massive hog, outweighing me five times over, he still obeyed these commands like a pet poodle.

True to Judge Taylor's description Traveller seemed to reason out problems. He knew to first tug loose a lace before stealing your shoe. He would also twist the faucet at the side of the house with his mouth to get at the cool water. (Ophelia often came home from her shopping to find the backyard flooded; Rankin finally had to unscrew the tap.) Then there were the football games. Rankin had an old leaky Rawlins which I used to throw around the yard with Peter Owens. A game developed in which if either of us dropped a pass the pig would grab the half deflated football in his teeth and race off. He soon learned how to up-end us with his snout and root the football out of our hands. Peter always suffered worst in this game, being so slight he was forever whisked off his feet. But this was a trick that would one day prove unfortunate for Traveller.

Rankin never took part in these games – though he always watched. One evening I remember him saying:

'You just keep treating him like a dog – it won't be so much fun when you find him in the freezer wrapped in brown paper.'

Comments like this had little effect on me, as I couldn't imagine anyone even suggesting such a thing. Mrs. Pierrepont might just as well skewer Shotzy and roast her over the barbecque.

Yet Rankin was less trusting of fate. Perhaps this was not surprising considering his young childhood. Nothing and no one could be totally relied upon – that was the lesson. Best to keep a manly distance as Judge Taylor advised. But this was not just so easy.

For one thing it soon became obvious that Rankin was avoiding pork. Ophelia had not noticed this at first – the bacon left untouched at breakfast, the chops forked onto my plate at dinner time. (I ate them gladly.) Then one night Ophelia made what once had been my brother's very favorite meal – ham steak and pineapple. Rankin could just not resist. He swallowed the meat hardly bothering to chew, then cleared his plate, soaking up the salty-sweet juice with a buttermilk biscuit. Later that night I listened outside the door as he made himself vomit in the upstairs bathroom.

But it was the incident with Megan Anderson that left him most exposed. The Andersons lived across Franklin Place in a large wooden ranch-style house. Bob Anderson was a jovial, pot-bellied East Texan – never without a joke. If Rankin and I saw him out in his front yard he'd bellow across the street:

'Circle the wagons, it's the Calhoun boys.'

Neither of us knew exactly what this meant but we'd smile and wave.

Anderson occasionally crossed paths with my father in business as he was an attorney representing the Livaudais, a family with large oil and gas holdings in Terrebonne Parish. But I think they also had a certain affinity for one another beyond business, both being Tulane-educated misfits in the rigid, name-conscious Uptown scene. 'Just a couple of hayseeds,' Anderson would say.

Both had also married McGehee's graduates. My mother was two years below Mrs. Anderson and they had known each other in the Junior League. She was a short, chubby woman with a dark golfer's tan and a deep gravelly voice from an excess of cigarettes and whiskey sours. Her name was Elspeth, though her friends called her Ep, and she hated Metairie almost as much as my mother had, but refused to move back Uptown unless it was to the Garden District.

The Andersons had three daughters. Laurel and Britain were the younger two, both small, quiet girls with striking brown eyes and matching page-boy haircuts. Mrs Anderson used to dress them in identical outfits, trying to pass the two off as twins. But Britain was actually the younger by a year.

Megan Anderson was the oldest daughter and looked nothing like her sisters – a tall dark-haired girl with a thin cheerless face and mean black eyes. I was always frightened of her – not that she paid me much mind. Megan attended

Sacred Heart Academy, an exclusive girls school on St Charles Avenue that seemed to infuse class consciousness into the lunch milk.

One afternoon the three of them appeared at our back gate. Rankin had gone to baseball practice and I was out in the yard playing football with Peter and Traveller.

'We've come to see your pig,' Megan announced through the fence.

I peered out the wooden slats. She stood in the driveway wearing a white Izod top and a short pleated tennis skirt. Her hair was pulled back and wound in a tight glossy braid, and she twirled a badminton racket in her hand.

'Are you going to let us in?'

'I'm really not supposed to,' I said.

Traveller was by then pressing his snout between the slats, sniffing out new odours – clean cotton blouses and moist Jr. Miss Sneakers. Laurel and Britain collapsed in giggles over this. Megan remained unsmiling.

'Where is your brother?'

I told her Rankin was out. She stood up on the tips of her toes, anyway, peering over the fence to see if I was lying. But only Peter was there – just in reach of the kitchen door.

'My cousin Jeffery is in your brother's class at St. Francis,' Megan then said.

'He told me your brother comes to school smelling like a pig.'

Laurel and Britain all but convulsed at this. Megan still didn't smile. I felt as though I ought to say something in Rankin's defense but nothing sprung to mind. Besides, I knew it was probably true. Megan didn't pursue the matter.

'Does your brother go to Valencia?' she then asked.

This struck me as an odd question. Valencia was an Uptown social club for young people, with a swimming pool, ping pong and pool tables, and a snack bar. Dance parties were held there every Tuesday night during the summer – strictly chaperoned.

I told her that Rankin wouldn't be caught dead at Valencia. Only much later did it occur to me that Megan might actually have a crush on my brother. Though it could hardly have mattered then as Rankin gave little thought to girls and certainly none to Megan Anderson.

Not having my brother to tease, Megan turned her attention to Traveller.

'Does it like to squirm about in the mud?'

'No,' I said. 'He hates the mud.'

This was, in fact, a lie. Traveller did enjoy the occasional roll on very warm days. But I didn't want to give Megan the satisfaction.

'It must eat a lot to be as fat as that.'

'Just slop. All the leftovers get dumped in a bucket and mixed up.'

'Sounds horrible. Does your maid do that?'

'Ophelia makes the food but Rankin does the slopping.'

'Well I guess that must be why he smells so bad.'

Had I been bigger I might have punched her. But I knew that Megan was not above beating me up and then spreading the fact throughout the neighborhood.

'Are you going to let me in?' She then demanded.

Ophelia had expressly forbidden allowing any other children in the yard with Traveller. I told Megan this.

'Do you always do what your maid says?' She replied.

Now I must admit that – unhitching the latch – I had at least half an idea what might happen. Laurel and Britain backed away. Megan squeezed through the narrow gap I held open.

First encounters always excited Traveller, new smells and textures. Here suddenly in the yard was Megan – like some undiscovered country. The pig pressed forward and thrust his moist snout straight up her tennis dress. Megan screamed blue murder and fell backwards into the dirt. Traveller thought this was wonderful. He charged forward and snuffled at her soft thighs. Megan began to holler and kick, clutching desperately at her skirt. But this seemed only to excite Traveller more.

In a panic I grabbed one of his rear legs and held tight. This restrained the pig long enough for Megan to scoot away a foot or so. She then drew back the badminton racket and swung it with all her strength. The blow landed with a sharp crack and sent Traveller screeching across the yard, tossing his head in agonised surprise.

Megan's screams had brought Ophelia hurrying out of the kitchen. She ran across the yard and reached down.

'It's okay now darling.'

But Megan pulled away.

'Don't you touch me.'

Laurel and Britain were howling outside the fence. Megan then stood up and staggered to the gate. She threw it open and whirled about.

'Tell your brother I hate him,' she screamed.

A few seconds passed as Laurel and Britain's cries receded across the street and vanished through the Anderson's front door. Ophelia grabbed my arm and yanked me into the house, up the stairs to my bedroom.

'You ain't coming out till Christmas.'

She then slammed shut the door. I ran to the window. Peter stood on the back stoop ossified in embarrassment. Traveller was nibbling calmly at his shoelaces.

'Is he hurt?'

Peter shook his head.

'Think you better go home now,' I said.

So without a word he ran to the fence and scrambled over the top. For a long time – hours it seemed – I sat staring out over the yard watching Traveller root through the dirt for insects, oblivious to the enormity of his crime. How could I even form the words to explain to my father what had happened.

Rankin returned from baseball practice. I heard him down in the kitchen talking to Ophelia, and slipped quickly under the bed remembering the last beating. But Rankin made no effort to find me when he came into the room. He pulled off his baseball uniform and threw his cleats into the closet.

'Hope you like bacon, Milo.'

This was all he said. I peered up from under the bed and saw he was crying. After a minute or so he wiped his face and went back down to the kitchen. I felt utterly miserable. Later that evening my father arrived home from the office and I expected at any moment to hear his footsteps on the stairs. But only Ophelia came up with my dinner on a tray. George had said little when she'd told him, and was now reading his newspaper. I had just started to feel a little better when the doorbell rang.

My father walked into the front hall and unlocked the door. Bob Anderson's loud voice echoed up the stairs.

'Sorry to bother you, George. Could we have a word?'

My father led him into the den. I slipped out to the top of the stairs and listened to the murmur of their conversation behind the closed door. It must have been nearly an hour before George stepped out into the hall again and called up the stairs.

Mr. Anderson smiled at me when I came into the room. He was sitting on the couch with a glass of scotch. His tie was pulled loose, and his jacket thrown over the arm of a chair. George closed the door.

'David, I want you to tell Mr. Anderson exactly what happened with Megan out in the backyard this afternoon.'

All that evening I'd rehearsed what to say. I stared across at my father's oxblood brogues and told them what happened – mostly it was the truth.

'Well, son, that's not exactly Megan's version of things,' said my father once I'd finished.

'She told her mother that you and Peter Owens invited her into our yard and grabbed her, then held her down so that the pig could . . .'

George seemed at a loss for words. He looked up at the ceiling in annoyance.

'. . . get at her.'

I was dumbfounded.

'But we never touched her. She fell down. Traveller just thought it was a game. I told her that nobody was allowed in the yard.'

'Don't lie to me now.'

Then Mr Anderson spoke for the first time.

'That's okay, George. Don't press him. Like I said it'd take more than David here and little Peter Owen to hold down Megan. She didn't have any business coming around here in the first place. But I just wanted to get the story straight.'

He rose from the couch and put on his jacket.

'I'm really sorry about this George. It's just that Ep was spitting blood.'

'No, she's every right to be angry. Tomorrow David will go over first thing after school and apologize.'

'That won't be necessary.'

'No, I insist.'

George walked Mr Anderson back over to his house, pausing a moment to look at Ep's rhododendrons. Then he strolled back across the street and took me straight into the study for a whipping. I was restricted to my room for the next week. But Rankin's fears for Traveller proved unfounded in the end. Later that night my father phoned Reives and made a definite arrangement. Traveller was to go to the farm for now.

But the trouble didn't end just then and there. Megan held to her version of events. Ep Anderson refused to believe her daughter could possibly lie about being violated by two eight-year-olds and a pig. So that night she phoned Mrs. Owens and demanded that Peter be punished. Mrs. Owens told her she would do no such thing and hung up.

Next Ep tried the school. Laurel and Britain both went to St Francis Xavier, so she phoned Sister Joan and threatened to pull her daughters from the school unless Peter and I were properly disciplined. Sister called us out of class for almost an hour of questioning in her office. Then both of us were given a week's detention – at least until Mrs. Owens stormed into the principal's office and threatened to pull Peter out of school unless Sister changed her mind and apologized for having overstepped her bounds. The trouble eventually blew over with nothing more serious than Ep Anderson's lasting enmity.

That Saturday morning I awoke to the sound of a loud engine idling at the side of the house. Rankin's bed was empty, and I heard voices down in the kitchen. On my way downstairs I paused at the window on the landing. Parked out in the driveway was a battered Ford pick-up truck – an old model from the 1940s with a boxed hood and shoulder-like front fenders. It was painted in a dull red primer, with scabs of rust blistering through the finish. An iron cattle trailer was hitched at the back.

But instead of Reives, another man stood in the kitchen talking with Ophelia. He was tall and thin, about age sixty, with light coffee-colored skin and grey wiry hair. A stiff cowboy hat was pushed back from his forehead, and he wore an easy, if slightly wry, smile.

'This is Mr Joe Dreux,' said Ophelia. 'He's taking Traveller back up to Buck Falaya. Reives wasn't feeling up to it this morning.'

'Pleased to meet you,' said Joe and winked as he grabbed my hand in a strong, leathery grip.

Rankin was out in the yard giving Traveller one last scrub down with the brush and hose. Joe turned and leaned against the door jamb.

'So this is how city pigs live. Thought it was only true in magazines.'

He then strolled out the door and across the yard to Traveller. The pig sniffed at his fingers.

'So you the one who raised this animal from a runt?'

Rankin nodded. Joe gave the pig a long appraising look and slapped him lightly on the haunch.

'Ain't he a fine one though. Can't say he's done much for the yard though.'

Rankin didn't smile.

'Will Mr. Reives feed him until we come up for the summer?'

'Think that's the plan,' said Joe. 'But don't you worry, I'll see old Traveller gets looked after.'

Later that morning Joe backed his trailer up the drive, close enough so that the ramp could be slid out to the open gate. He put a rope harness on Traveller. But Rankin had little trouble coaxing the pig into the trailer with a peeled banana.

Joe swung the tailgate shut. Traveller grunted in agitation and banged his snout against the heavy iron bars. My father pressed a ten dollar bill into Joe's hand as he climbed into the cab. The old Ford roared to life. Rankin and I followed it down the driveway and watched from the frontyard as the trailer bounced away up Franklin Place.

It was then that Traveller graced the neighborhood with one last offering. It tumbled out the tailgate and splattered across the clean hot pavement.

Chapter 6

A massive live oak grows in a bend of the gravel road that leads up to the porch of our house at Buck Falaya. The trunk must be fifteen or so feet in circumference, with a thick pedestal of roots spreading out from the base like a nest of tangled pythons. Its canopy is as broad as a revival tent, and some of the branches have grown so long and heavy that they dip back into the earth, and have taken root.

For the first few summers at the farm I used to spend hours a day up that tree. Rankin viewed this as proof postive of my Milo tendencies. There was one branch in particular that reached out over the road in a gentle arc. It was so broad that I could walk upright along its surface hardly needing to balance. It seemed to me the perfect place from which an ambush might have been launched, and I could imagine long columns of Yankee soldiers marching underneath unaware of the danger above.

One June afternoon while up in my tree I spotted a kid

about Rankin's age loitering over at our gate. He was short and fat, with shaggy blond hair, his sun-burned cheeks so plump they gave his eyes a pinched oriental look. He wore a dirty, blue cotton shirt, vastly oversized and tucked into a pair of drooping khaki scout trousers.

For nearly half an hour I watched him – balancing up and down the iron bars of the cattle guard, throwing gravel at our mail box, picking off birds and squirrels with an imaginary shotgun. Every few minutes he'd look toward the house as though expecting someone to appear on the porch.

Eventually he seemed to grow tired of waiting and began to saunter up the drive, whistling. I waited until he was almost underneath the tree before I called out. He stopped and turned completely around twice. I called out again and he finally looked up.

'Think I didn't see you up there?' He said.

'No.' I replied.

'Well, I did. All the way from the end of the road.'

I found this hard to credit, but didn't say so. The kid took a few more steps out from under the branch to get a better look at me.

'How old are you?' He demanded.

'Nine.'

'And how old's your brother?'

'Twelve.'

'See that's what I thought. My momma was wrong – again.'

He said this as though the point had been well argued and then, almost as afterthought, asked:

'So you want to see some baby possums?'

'Some what?'

'Possums. Ain't you ever seen a possum.'

'Sure,' I replied, not adding that it was only a dead one once on the side of the road. The kid narrowed his eyes dubiously.

'You can ask your brother to come too.'

So I climbed down from the tree and ran to the back of the house. Rankin was out doing his requisite two hours of painting on the barn. Traveller watched dejectedly through the rails of his pen. Most often the pig had the run of the place, but not during painting as he had a fondness for white lead Sherwin-Williams and would lick it wet off the walls.

Rankin put down his brush and followed me around to the front of the house. The kid stood leaning against the trunk of the big oak.

'Bout time,' he said and then, taking a step foward, tripped and fell heavily onto the roots.

'You okay?' Asked Rankin.

The kid struggled to his feet and dabbed at a bleeding elbow with his shirt tail.

'Oh it's just a scrape.'

He then wiped his right hand across the back of his trousers and held it out to my brother.

'James-Tyler-Fendleson-the-Third.'

Rankin grasped it uncertainly and introduced himself.

'Guess you already met Milo,' he then added.

But before I could protest that this was not my real name Tyler was already grinning. He still calls me Milo to this day.

The possums were in a corn field behind Tyler's house. Just beyond our cattle guard, a narrow trail cut through the woods, one of Tyler's many shortcuts. He looked back to make sure we'd followed. Then turning ahead he began to whistle – a sort of bouncy marching tune.

'Hear that,' he said, breaking off. 'Just made it up in my head. Now I got 13 made-up whistle songs. Want to hear another one?'

Tyler licked his lips and began to whistle again – a nondescript tune that sounded exactly like the first. Rankin and I stared at our feet trying not to make each other laugh.

Soon the trail emerged at a field edge. Rows of tall green cornstalks swayed in the hot breeze. Tyler paused.

'Now ya'll walk right behind me, Indian-style, and watch out for traps.'

He pointed to the base of a nearby cornstalk. Buried just under the sandy soil was a small round disc of dull steel, surrounded by an oval of serated teeth.

Tyler led us through the corn rows as though the field were mined. He pointed out a halfdozen other traps that his father had set to catch the possums and racoons that ate his corn. A dirt track cut through the middle of the field and led up to a large white house about a quarter mile away. A dog barked incessantly. Tyler crossed over the track without comment. We had only gone a few yards more when he suddenly raced ahead.

'Yep, still here.'

It took a few seconds to figure out exactly what it was Tyler pointed to. A large possum lay across one of the corn rows, its grey fur matted with blood, the long fleshy tail curled and rigid. The trap had split open the animal's skull. A blanket of flies covered its head and the surrounding soil, which was sodden with blood and brains.

Tyler reached down and pulled at the tail.

'You see em?' He asked.

Just then a tiny rat-like creature emerged from a large slit in the animal's belly, followed by another. My first thought was that the possum was being eaten from the inside out. My throat tightened and I felt my stomach begin to churn. Even Rankin looked horrified.

Tyler grinned at our reaction.

'Bet you never seen a pouch baby before,' he said. 'There's two more inside her.'

Rankin knelt down in the dirt for a closer look.

'Are you gonna keep them?' He asked.

'No way. My Daddy hates possums. What you think all them traps are for?'

'What'll he do with them?'

'Drown em probably. That's what he did to the kittens in the barn.'

Tyler then poked at one of the babies with a dried cornstalk.

'They'd just die anyway.'

That night I dreamt of possums – small warm creatures crawling in my hands, eating blackberries. Later I was awakened by the sound of heavy rain pounding on the tin roof. It was long before dawn. Lying in the dark I tried to imagine those blind faces, groping over that dead animal in the wet corn. I decided to return in the morning with a cardboard box and take them to the barn. There I'd raise them on milk and table scraps. Then once the babies had grown large enough, I'd release them into the wild again – just like *Born Free*. Satisfied with this resolve I drifted back to sleep.

In the morning I awoke to find James-Tyler-Fendleson-the-Third standing in the doorway of our bedroom. He was wearing the same dirty blue shirt and khakis.

'Hey,' he whispered, seeing my eyes open.

'Ya'll's maid told me to come on in. It's already eight o'clock. Do you get up this late every day?'

He sat on the end of my bed and looked over at Rankin who was still sound asleep.

'Nobody has to get me up. Six thirty and boom I'm awake.'

Then lowering his voice, he said,

'Guess what. My daddy didn't drown those possums after all. He killed em with the hoe. Crushed their heads – one by one.'

For some reason a vivid picture of this formed in my mind – a tall faceless farmer with heavy arms pressing down on a wooden shaft, each tiny skull cracking with a soft pop. It seemed cruel and brutal to me. But Tyler looked unbothered. I thought maybe I was just being soft.

Ophelia invited Tyler to have breakfast with us that morning. She was making pancakes – our Saturday treat. The smell of hot oil and sweet buttermilk batter filled the house. Tyler at first politely refused when she offered him a stack.

'No thank you mam. I had my breakfast already – 6:30 am with my daddy.'

'Not even one?,' said Ophelia.

'No mam, I really shouldn't.'

But of couse he did – a broad stack of three pancakes smothered in butter and maple syrup.

'Aunt Jemima's the best,' said Tyler, his mouth full and sticky. 'My Daddy only eats cane syrup; it's like swallowing pine sap.'

'So is your Daddy a farmer?' Ophelia asked.

'Yes mam. We own a thousand acres – just across the fence.'

Tyler pointed his knife toward the window.

'There've been Fendlesons on that land for over a 120 years.'

'Really.'

'Yes mam, since before the Civil War.'

Tyler forked another pancake onto his plate. Ophelia passed him the butter.

'So do you plan to be a farmer like your Daddy?'

'No mam, I'm gonna be a herpetologist.'

Tyler glanced around table for any sign of recognition.

'A herpetologist,' said Ophelia slowly. 'Now I won't even pretend I know what that is.'

'Herpetology is the scientific study of reptiles and amphibians,' said Tyler. 'You know like turtles and frogs and lizards. My special interest is snakes.'

'Lord, lord. Whatever for?'

'I just like 'em.'

Tyler then glanced over at us.

'I got nine snakes at home out back of the barn.'

'Bet your momma's just thrilled about that,' said Ophelia.

'Oh, no mam.'

Tyler grinned over his empty plate.

Later that morning Rankin brought the leftovers out to Traveller. Tyler and I sat on the railings of the pen watching Rankin struggle to keep the pig's head out of the slop bucket.

'Greedy thing,' said Tyler.

Rankin pretended not to hear this and spread the slop with his hand.

'My uncle raises hogs over in Talisheek,' said Tyler.

'He kills one for Christmas every year, and then he sends us a big side of smoked bacon. Boy is it good. Nothing like you get at the Winn Dixie.'

I turned to him.

'Don't talk like that in front of the p-i-g.'

But it was actually Rankin that concerned me most.

Tyler persisted:

'It don't understand nothing.'

He then leaned over the fence and chanted:

'Bacon, pork chop, crackling, sausage.'

Traveller took no notice, having now climbed over the edge of the trough to get at the last traces of slop at the bottom. Tyler giggled.

'See.'

But my brother was not smiling. Traveller now having licked the trough clean began to sniff at Tyler's shoes. There was an awkward silence. Then Rankin picked up the bucket and strode off toward the pump at the side of the barn. Tyler leapt off the railings to follow.

'Sure is getting hot,' he said, his short legs trying to keep pace with Rankin's.

'Ya'll want to go for a swim at the river. I know a really good spot. I got some chores to do, but I could come back this afternoon.'

He was almost pleading.

Rankin cleaned out the bucket. He then filled it again with water and carried it back to wash the trough. Tyler jogged along side him.

'Is it far?' Rankin finally asked.

'No sir-ree.'

Tyler reappeared later that day still wearing the same blue shirt, but the khakis had been exchanged for a pair of jeans, cut off in ragged edges just above the knees. He was wearing a pair of filthy blue deck shoes and had a Yogi Bear beach towel draped over one shoulder. Rankin and I were waiting on the front porch in our new matching summer swim suits, both with stretch polyester belts and brass-effect 'anchor' buckles. Ophelia had ordered them from J.C. Penney's.

Tyler made no mention of the suits then – just grinned as we came down the steps. Ophelia waved from the porch as we set off across the pasture. It was a dry, hot afternoon. The cattle had retreated to the shade. The ground was as hard as fired clay, and the red dust of the pasture flew up from the back of our sneakers as we walked.

'I been thinking about your pig,' said Tyler, wiping away a trickle of sweat from his forehead.

'Not that I'm much of a judge of hogs, but I bet that if you fattened up that pig . . .'

'You mean Traveller,' I said.

'. . . yea, if you fattened up old Traveller you could enter him in the Fair. He might just win a ribbon.'

'What fair?' asked Rankin.

'The St Tammany Parish Fair. It's in August. They got a livestock show. Last year I saw all kinds of pigs. One of em was as big as a VW.'

'Our pig's not that big,' said Rankin.

'That don't matter. See they judge them by their age and breed. My uncle told me. Size ain't all they look for. They got to be healthy – there's a whole big list of things. Ya'll want to hear my plan?'

Streams of sweat poured down Tyler's face in his excitement.

'Lots of houses around Buck Falaya just throw out their leftovers. We could go around collecting it and feed it to the pig. It'd be sort of like training a prize fighter. Then you could enter him in the Fair. My momma already says she'll let us have our leftovers.'

I found it hard to imagine any leftovers at all in the Fendleson household after watching Tyler at breakfast. But the idea excited me; I could already picture Traveller on the front page of the *St Tammany Farmer*.

'Joe Dreux did say he had good form,' said Rankin.

'Anybody can see that,' Tyler replied.

'Suppose it couldn't hurt to try.'

'It never hurts to try.'

'Okay.'

'Okay then!'

Tyler danced ahead, kicking up a rooster tail of orange dust.

A quarter of mile from the house we reached the far edge of the pasture. Beyond it, across a tangle of blackberry bushes, was a thick wood. Tyler ducked through a small opening in the briars and told us to keep a look out for 'black runners'.

'Fastest snake in Louisiana.'

I never bothered to ask if it was poisonous or not: the trail was too narrow for escape. But after a few yards the thicket began to open up, and it was though we'd stepped through some secret passage. Never before had I been in such a forest – the diffuse olivine light from the high canopy, the air cool and heavy in contrast to the sun-burnt fields. It was a mixed forest of long leaf pine, massive oaks, beech, dogwood and ash. Many of the trees looked ancient – their trunks knotted and tumorous. There was hardly a sound, only the slight rustle of leaves when the wind stirred the high branches. I felt vaguely out of place and a little spooked.

Eventually the ground began to drop off and the trail grew uneven, winding through sandy hollows and hummocks, the remnants of old abandoned river courses. A few hundred yards further we reached the Bogue Falaya river.

Tyler led us along the high, densely wooded bank. Sunlight fell in scattered patches on the water, which was stained a clear amber from the red clay. Soon we reached a sandy bend in the river where a tree had fallen across the main channel, creating a deep-water pool. A knotted rope, tied to an overhanging branch of a large live oak, swayed across the surface. On the far side of the bend, a steep cutbank of moist clay dropped steeply into the water.

Tyler peeled off his shirt and waded into the river to grab the rope. He then climbed back onto the bank and draped it over his shoulders before clambering up a set of wooden rungs nailed into the tree trunk. These rose to a small platform made from three pine planks fixed into the base of the overhanging branch. Tyler pulled the rope between his legs and leapt out into the air.

'Don't forget to write,' he yelled.

The branch groaned as he sailed far out over the river and dropped like a stone into the pool. He dog-paddled back to the shallows and leapt up to catch the swinging rope. Next Rankin had a turn.

'Just make sure you let go the first time,' said Tyler, 'else you'll kill yourself swinging back into the tree.'

Rankin stepped off the platform without a moment's hesitation. His toes skimmed the surface of the water as he flew out over the Bogue Falaya, nearly reaching the clay bank on the far side.

Tyler caught the rope as it swung back into the tree. He held it out to me.

'Have a go, Milo.'

By then my initial eagerness for a turn had already begun to fade. I took the rope and began to climb the slippery wet rungs. Reaching the top step, I hugged the worn bark of the trunk and inched my way around to the platform.

Now the base of this oak stood nine or ten feet above the river bank, making the platform nearly twenty feet above the surface of the water. To me it seemed at least a hundred.

I barely managed to pull the rope between my thighs.

'Come on, Milo,' Rankin shouted.

'Jump already!'

My legs began to shake uncontrollably.

'Jump, dammit!'

But nothing could induce me to let go. I opened my knees and the rope fell away.

'Jesus Christ. What a baby.'

I climbed back down the wooden steps and sat over on the bank. Rankin and Tyler then spent the next hour taking turns at the swing, howling like Apaches. I felt an utter coward.

Eventually Tyler climbed out of the water and sat up in the sand beside me. He reached for his beach towel and unrolled it at his feet. Inside was a battered Tom & Jerry pencil case, the contents of which Tyler emptied onto the towel – a pocket knife, some pennies and nickels, a tattered library card and what appeared to be a dried-out crow's foot. There was also a tin cigar cylinder containing a parcel of tissue paper. Carefully drying his hands, Tyler unwrapped the paper and pulled out a half-smoked True Green cigarette and two kitchen matches.

'Want a puff,' he called out to Rankin, who was still in the river.

'Where'd you get it from?'

'My momma's purse.'

'Won't she miss it?'

'No chance. She smokes like a tractor.'

Rankin climbed up the bank and took the cigarette from Tyler, holding it to his lips as though it were a lit firecracker. He took a shallow puff and handed it back.

'Nothing like a cig after a swim,' Tyler sighed. He then held it out towards me.

'No thanks,' I said, adding rather hopefully. 'Ophelia smells everything.'

Tyler smoked the cigarette until it had burned down below the filter. He then smothered it in the sand and buried the evidence.

'So have ya'll moved up here for good?' He asked.

'No, just for the summer,' replied Rankin.

'That ain't very long.'

'Twelve and a half more weeks.'

'Be over before you know it. So what happens to your house when you go.'

'It's just locked up until the next visit. Mr. Reives looks after it.'

'Gilbert Reives! You must be joking,' said Tyler.

'What's wrong with him?'

'Besides being a thief and a drunk?'

'How do you know that?' Rankin asked.

'Everybody knows. He buys his bottles from Marslan's. Starts drinking in the morning and by the afternoon he's smashed.'

'Have you ever seen him drunk?'

'Just about every day. He sits out on the porch in his rocking chair. Sometimes he yells things at me when I walk past after school.'

'Like what?'

'I don't know . . . like stuff about it being chow time. I hate his guts.'

'Well I can't say I like him much either,' said Rankin. 'My father pays him to help out around the farm – but he never does anything except ride around on his tractor.'

'Well I'd just make sure he don't help himself to some of your tools. My daddy won't let him near our property. One morning he caught Reives taking one of the wheelbarrows out of our shed. Gilbert said he was just borrowing it for an hour or two cause his had a flat tire. Then other tools started disappearing.'

'Can't you do anything?'

'Well my daddy keeps saying that one night he just might have a peek over in Reives' shed. But momma is afraid he'd get shot.'

'Doesn't he have a daughter?'

'You mean Alice the Goon. She's nearly grown-up and still plays with dolls'.

'Dolls?'

'Yep. There's loads of em in that house. Everybody says she's simple.'

'So what happened to her mother?'

'Oh she died a long time ago, before I was born. Reives probably did her in. I heard my momma say once he used to beat her up when he got drunk. He still knocks old Gooney around.'

'Why doesn't she just leave?'

'How should I know?'

Tyler stood up and pulled on his shirt.

'Ya'll thirsty? Lets go up to Marslan's for a rootbeer.'

James-Tyler-Fendleson-the-Third had an insatiable craving for Rex Rootbeer. He spent at least half his weekly allowance on Rex forays to Marslan's General Grocery up by the bridge. Ray Marslan – Buck Falaya's only storekeeper – was a wiry, nervous man with an overactive thyroid, his exophthalmic eyes perpetually on alert for shoplifters. In the top pocket of his shirt he kept a black, oily comb which he'd run compulsively through his hair every time he made a sale.

Marslan's was really no more than a shack. The shelves

were sparsely stocked, as most people in Buck Falaya did their main shopping in Covington or Folsom. There was usually some stale bread and a few dusty boxes of cereal. Ray was loathe to discard stock. Tyler swears that the same can of Green Giant Spinach and Niblet Corn has stood on a shelf for the last sixteen years.

Most of Marslan's trade was in milk, soft drinks, beer, hard liquor, cigarettes and newspapers. He also sold 'Men's Magazines' which he kept behind the counter tucked in a wooden rack for decency sake – though occasionally you might glimpse a nipple peeking through the slats.

King-size bottles of Rex, Coke-a-Cola, Nehi Grape and Seven-Up were stored in a deep casket-like refrigerator. A wooden crate was pushed up against it so that small kids could reach over the side. Each time I went to fish out a bottle from that fridge I had to suppress an irrational fear of toppling in and the heavy lid slamming shut.

But Tyler assured me this would never happen.

'Ray'd be afraid you might drink a free Coke before you suffocated.'

A two-cent deposit on bottles meant that we had to sit out in the shade of the gas island to drink our sodas. The air was still and hot. An old fat Labrador trotted over from across the road and sniffed at our shoes, then collapsed in the shade and began to lick his genitals. Tyler snorted:

'Taste good, Sam? That's Mr Wingfield's dog. Can always depend on Sam to lick his nuts in polite company.'

Finishing his wash, the dog stretched out at our feet with a groan and fell instantly asleep, his tongue lolling out onto the dusty gravel.

I sat happily with my cold grape drink, listening to Tyler and Rankin debate TV westerns. Soon I forgot my humiliation at the rope swing. Tyler began to throw gravel at the wooden sign for the Liberty Baptist Church. Sam's tail wagged on impulse, thumping in the dust. We then heard the sound of a distant motorcycle, a low rumble approaching on the long stretch of road before the bridge. Tyler jumped to his feet.

'What's wrong with you?' Rankin asked.

'Let's go back inside now.'

'Why?'

But Tyler was already making for the screen door into Marslan's. The rumble grew louder and I half expected to see a giant Harley or a BSA. But it was only a small Honda – little more than a scooter – that raced over the bridge, its rider ridiculously oversized, his knees nearly touching the handle bars.

Just as the motorcyle passed Marslan's the rider spotted us and slammed his heel to the foot brake. The tires locked and moaned across the hot asphalt, and the bike slid off the road into the gravel. Tyler pushed through the screen door.

'What's the big deal?' Rankin asked.

'Is he coming?'

'Yea, I think so.'

'Wonderful.'

Tyler hurried to the rear of the store and hid behind a revolving rack of fishing lures next to the magazine stand.

'Who is he?'

'Bone.'

'Who?'

'Frank Bone,' Tyler whispered harshly. 'He's after me.'

'What for?'

'It's a long story. Is he still coming?'

'Looks like it.'

'That's just great.'

The Honda coasted up in front of the grocery, a 100 cc with no muffler, idling like an earthmover. No other name could have been more apt for the kid who killed the engine and climbed off that bike. Frank Bone was a tall, pencil-thin teenager with a long face that simply boiled with acne. Even his twig-like arms were dotted with pimples. He wore jeans and a tight black tee-shirt with a pack of Marlboros rolled up in one sleeve. His greasy hair was swept back in a duck tail; his eyes hidden by cheap plastic sunglasses.

Bone walked into the store and peered down the aisle, lifting his shades.

'Do I see Turd-the-Third back there?'

He strolled to the magazine stand and glanced around the rack of spinners and rubber worms.

'What you hiding from?'

'Nothing,' replied Tyler.

'Not hiding from me, are you?'

'Why should I?'

Bone poked a finger at his chest.

'Don't play dumb you little shit. Better put em back.'

'I don't know what you're talking about.'

'The hell you don't.'

He shoved Tyler hard into the magazine stand, scattering a pile of *Outdoor Life*. Marslan shouted from the counter:

'You boys stop that in here. Get on out Frank, unless you plan on buying something. You pick up them magazines Tyler.'

'Just leaving sir,' said Bone. He then leaned close to Tyler and whispered.

'Better put em back or I'll break your arm.'

'Clear on out son,' Marslan yelled.

Bone waved to the counter as he walked out. Tyler and Rankin then bent down to gather up the magazines.

'What's he talking about?' Rankin asked.

'I'll tell you later.'

For the next half-hour Tyler stood watching out Marslan's doorway. Then suddenly, without warning, he dashed out across the parking lot and ran hard up the road. Rankin and I didn't catch him until the entrance to Fendleson Farm. Tyler gasped:

'Think we're okay now.'

'Why's he after you?' Rankin asked again.

'Cause he thinks I stole something from him.'

'Did you?'

'No. I mean I didn't steal it. I found it. He stole it in first place.'

'What is it.'

'Ya'll come by tomorrow and maybe I'll show you. I'm late for dinner now.'

Tyler ran up the drive and waved before vanishing into one of his trails. By then it was nearly six in the evening. Rankin and I began to jog down the gravel road home. It was still blazing hot – despite the hour. I was tired and hungry. Nearing the cattle guard I began to walk again. Rankin shouted:

'Hurry up, Milo.'

It was then, just passed the Reives' front gate, that we heard a voice call out:

'Stranger than fiction.'

Or at least that's what it sounded like – hoarse and barely recognizable. At first I could only see the smoke of his cigarette drifting out from the shadow of the porch into the low sunlight. Rankin stopped and peered over the fence.

'Pardon?'

Gilbert rose out of his rocking chair and stumbled off the porch.

'Come on out back. I got something ya'll'd be interested in.'

Rankin looked at his watch and sighed. Reives shouted:

'Ya'll coming?'

We followed reluctantly around the side of the house. Though it seemed hardly possible, the shack was even more run-down than it looked from the road. Not a speck of paint remained on the wood siding, and a few of the panels had rotted away exposing the timber frame beneath. None of the windows had screens, and more than a couple of panes were shattered and taped over with cardboard.

Out back the yard was cluttered with junk metal – broken farm tools, a rusting box spring mattress. Behind the storage shed an old Ford engine hung on chains from a sagging child's swing set. Reives stood by a row of timber and chicken wire cages that extended along one side of the shed. Crowded inside were dozens of black and white patched rabbits, listless in the afternoon heat. Rankin and I peered into the cages, pushing our fingers through the wiring to touch the soft fur. But Reives was impatient.

'Them's just rabbits.'

His hand was resting on a much larger cage, the front of which was covered with a dirty wool blanket. He waited until we were both standing next to him.

'Now you won't see one of these in a million,' he said and threw back the blanket.

Cowering at the back of the cage was an albino racoon blinded by the sudden stream of sunlight. It was a small animal, probably less than a year old. Its eyes and snout were a pale pink, its fur a yellowish white. A large patch was missing from one shoulder, exposing pink, scabby flesh underneath. The cage was filthy, the floor plastered in brown droppings. Reives seemed not to notice this, or that the water bowl had overturned.

'You know a man offered me two hundred dollars for this animal,' he said. 'Turned him down cold.'

'How did you get it?' Rankin asked.

'Caught him in one of my traps. But don't you expect me to say where.'

Reives grinned and tapped the side of his nose.

'So what makes it white?' I asked.

'Just a freak of nature. Only God knows.'

But by then I had already begun to lose interest in the animal – which seemed to me rather ugly and pathetic. I wandered back over to one of the rabbit cages. Rankin peered closer through the wire.

'Looks sick to me.'

Reives' grin vanished.

'What do you mean, sick?'

'Just looks kind of mangy and sick. I don't think it's good for it being cooped up in the dark like that.'

Reives leaned back against the cage and regarded my brother with a thin smile.

'So what makes you the expert on racoons?'

'I never said I was an expert.'

'Them nuns teach you about racoons down in New Orleans?'

'No sir.'

'Oh I bet they teach you lots – them Sisters.'

Reives jerked the blanket back down. He then staggered over to the cage where I stood. Near the front a large rabbit nestled in a bed of stale smelling wood chips.

'Got a young buck there,' said Reives. 'Let's have a look.'

He opened the cage door and grabbed the rabbit by the ears. It took no more than a instant – his large hand closed round the neck and twisted it with a soft snap.

'Best eating at this age,' he said. 'You take this one home and have your maid cook it up for you.'

Rankin and I stared dumbfounded at the limp creature in his hands. To me it seemed inconceivable that something so warm and alive could be so suddenly dead. Reives shouted to the house:

'Alice!'

A moment later the kitchen door opened and a young woman appeared on the stoop. She must have been watching us all along.

Reives held the rabbit up by the ears.

'Put this in a paper bag for these boys' dinner.'

Alice hurried over and took the carcass without looking up at her father. She was a tall girl, thin and round shouldered, with long gangly arms. A loose plait of wiry ginger hair fell down her back, and her face was pale and covered in freckles. Walking back to the house she paused at the kitchen steps – as though about to say something – but then went quickly inside. Reives stared after her a moment.

'You boys wait here,' he muttered and disappeared through the back door.

All was silent. A few minutes later Alice reappeared carrying a rolled-up A&P bag. She silently handed it to Rankin – her eyes fixed to the ground. But as we turned to leave she glanced up with a frail smile and whispered:

'Come by anytime you like.'

Chapter 7

Sunday mornings at Buck Falaya passed with a sort of sweltering torpor. Ophelia would have us up and dressed for Mass before breakfast – scratchy linen suits, cotton shirts with tight collars and ties, stiff black leather shoes. Then she'd stand by the kitchen table as we choked down warm eggs and biscuits.

'I'm not having no grumbling guts next to me.'

No matter how early Ophelia might turn us out, Rankin always managed somehow to be late. Either he'd break a shoe lace or dribble egg down his tie or use too much Brylcream. Invariably I'd be left sweating out in the hot Buick until Ophelia bustled him out through the front door.

'Got to leave a crack in the window with Milo out here,' he'd say. 'Else we'll get SPCA on us.'

Ophelia would ignore him and gun the car.

'Forgive me Lord,' she'd mutter and tear out of the drive at high speed.

Being Roman Catholic didn't set us much apart from the inhabitants of Buck Falaya. Though Baptist, the hamlet lay on the lowermost fringes of the Bible Belt. In fact, if one were to draw a border it might run just south of Fendleson Farm heading west for the state capital at Baton Rouge. Here, Protestants and Creole Catholics regarded each other – on the whole – with tolerant suspicion. Local evangelicals casted happily for lapsed Mass-goers. Even the Ku Klux Klan was less rabid on the subject of papistry – though they more than made up for it on other fronts.

About ten miles south of Buck Falaya was a Benedictine Abbey and seminary college known as St. Albans. Here young men, most of them from distant Cajun towns like Thibodaux and Lafayette, trained to be priests. Here also to the chapel of the Abbey Ophelia hurled us to Mass.

The chapel was built in the 1920s, though the college is much older. Across the high walls and in the vaulted ceilings are colorful murals in which the saints mingle with ordinary people in modern dress – farmers, laborers, teachers, nurses. I can remember half-expecting to find the face of my mother among all those figures, taking so literally as I did Big Mom's assurances that Margot Aubry regularly interceded with the Holy on our behalf.

Rankin had even spotted a pig on the back wall – part of a farmyard tableau – though not the same breed as Traveller he informed us.

'Looks a bit like a Tamworth,' he whispered, 'though I wouldn't bet my rosary on it.'

Rankin hated Mass. Either he'd fidget compulsively or drop off to sleep, his head lolling back against the hardwood pew with an echoing crack. But I was much taken with the quiet grandour of the chapel, the deep, mild tone of the seminarians at their Latin prayers and hymns. My ambition that summer was to become a monk – to wear a brown robe and sandles and spend the day tending the vegetable garden or sweeping the chapter house. I'd eat 'simply' and sleep in

a tiny cell with a block of wood as a pillow. My notions of
monastic life derived from a chapter on the Dark Ages in
my *Golden Book of World History*. I remember being vaguely
disappointed to learn that the Brothers at St. Albans had a
TV room and a recreation hall with ping-pong tables.

Rankin's response to all this was predictable.

'Milo the monkee.'

That Sunday we paid our first visit to the Fendleson's. Tyler
lived in a large, two-storey wooden farmhouse with a broad,
well-watered lawn, bordered from the corn rows by a split
rail fence. A sizeable barn and grain silo stood a few hundred
yards beyond, along with a large machinery shed with a
corrugated roof. Near the back door of the house was a kennel
with a concrete run enclosed by a high chain-link fence – the
permanent home of the Fendleson's wooden-headed Irish
Setter, Charlie Brown. This dog could not breath without
barking, and rarely – if ever – left his kennel. Last time
Charlie Brown escaped he had not stopped running until a
neighbor found him wandering in traffic out on the Folsom
Highway.

Our arrival that afternoon transported Charlie Brown
beyond barking, to a sort of choked bay. Tyler soon appeared at the back door and launched a tattered baseball
at the animal, which glanced off the kennel fence and into
the yard.

'Shut up, you idiot.'

Charlie Brown paused in sudden confusion – that being
a ball and he being a dog after all. But the inspiration passed
in an instant.

'Ya'll come around by the barn,' Tyler shouted over the
noise. 'and see my snakes.'

A stout red-haired woman stood at the kitchen window,
waving a dish towel as we passed around the back of
the house.

'We can see you fine mom,' Tyler shouted.

He then muttered under his breath:

'See what I have to put up with.'

Tyler kept his snakes in a dusty tack room off the side of the barn. A set of wooden shelves had been built along one wall and lined with glass aquariums of various sizes. Screen lids were fitted over the tanks and weighed down with bricks.

Tyler tapped at one of the larger aquariums, setting off a loud rattle. Nothing was visible in the deep bed of pine needles lining the bottom of the cage.

'You got a rattlesnake in there?' Rankin asked.

Tyler grinned and lifted off the screen lid. The rattling grew louder as he reached in and began to rummage through the pine straw. He then pulled out a long, glossy black snake covered with small yellow specks. I retreated to the door.

'Don't worry, he ain't poisonous,' said Tyler. 'Just a king snake. He only shakes his tail to make you think he's a rattler.'

True enough, the tail continued to vibrate soundless in the air, yet the snake seemed unperturbed as it coiled slowly around Tyler's arm, a thin red tongue flicking out, testing the air.

'Don't get many rattlesnakes around here,' said Tyler. 'Only pigmy rattlers and I've never even seen one. Not like over in western Louisiana where you get the big canebrake rattlers. Boy that'd be some catch.'

Tyler unwound the reptile from his arm and laid it back in the tank. He then gave us the full tour of his collection – a tangle of baby ribbon snakes, a brightly colored corn snake, a grass snake, a ratsnake, a hognosed snake, a watersnake – actually two of these, both lying in a pool of dirty water. Each reptile had its own miniature habitat made with straw or gravel and sticks and spanish moss.

On the end of one shelf stood a large pickle jar, half filled

with water, in which a dozen or so frogs floated dejectedly.
Tyler opened the lid and grabbed the fattest one, which he
then dropped into the watersnake aquarium. The larger of
the two struck instantly – swallowing the frog whole. We
stood watching for a minute or so as the motionless lump
crept down the reptile's gullet.

Tyler by then had shown us every tank but one – a
small aquarium filled with dried leaves on the top shelf. A
cardboard sign was taped to the side, with the message:

'Dangerous: handle only with permission of JTF III.'

'Is that one up there poisonous?' I asked.

'Not exactly,' Tyler replied with a grin.

He then quietly shut the door, and wedged an old chair
beneath the knob. Standing on a pine stool he slid the
aquarium off the shelf and handed it down to Rankin.

'You keep a look out the window Milo and make sure my
momma don't come out.'

'What's in there? Why can't I see?'

'Just do it,' snapped Rankin.

So I stood over by the grimy window and stared out at
the house. Tyler dug through the dry leaves in the tank. I
glanced back over my shoulder. This time it wasn't a snake
he pulled out, but a white envelope.

'Keep watching,' said Tyler.

He and Rankin huddled over the floor blocking my
view. Nothing was said for a moment or two. Then Rankin
moaned:

'That's sick.'

Tyler began to giggle.

'Christ sake. Where'd you get these?'

I tried to see over their shoulders.

'What's sick?'

'Turn around Milo,' Rankin hissed.

Tyler then leaned forward.

'Did you see this one – Dominique et Prince. Et means 'and' in French. I looked it up.'

Rankin shook his head.

'No way. That's just a camera trick.'

But Tyler only laughed.

'Here Prince, here boy.'

I stepped away from the window.

'Let me have a look.'

Rankin swung around.

'Get your ass back over to that window.'

But Tyler held out his hand.

'Aw let him see one. Else he might tell on us.'

He then tossed to me what looked like a baseball card.

'Eat it up Milo.'

The photo was in black and white, taken from the rear. The woman was on top of the man, glancing back over one shoulder, her back arched. A black bar covered her eyes, and her teeth were clenched in what I thought could only be agony. No man could be so large. It was absurd; simply not to be believed. Rankin snatched the photo from my hand.

'Satisfied.'

It was as though I'd been slapped. Few moments in my life have been just as clearly defining as that one. I felt the urge to vomit. Tyler grinned:

'Think he'd like to see Prince now?'

'No!' said Rankin. He then flicked through the other cards.

'So is this what that guy Bone was looking for?'

'Yep.'

'How did you get these?'

'Found em in an old shack out by the power lines.'

'You found those pictures?'

'Well sort of. Greg Salter showed me – he's Frank Bone's cousin. Probably got the shit kicked out him for it, too.'

'Are they Bone's?'

'Do you see his name on 'em anywhere?'

Tyler then slipped the cards back into the envelope and buried it again among the leaves in the tank. He stood up on the stool and replaced the aquarium on the shelf.

'Like the hiding place? My momma'd sooner die than stick her hand in there.'

Mrs. Fendleson later invited us in for lemonade. Miss Sis – as we knew her – was short and square, with a plain round face and large brillant blue eyes. She'd once been a teacher at Folsom Elementary but had given up the job to marry Tyler Senior. I can't imagine that it was a particularly satisfying marriage.

Mr Fendleson was much older, a large quiet man whose interests extended little beyond the boundaries of his farm. He wore an old felt hat and walked with a stout bamboo cane, as some years before he'd fallen from a hay truck and badly damaged a leg. Never once can I recall the man smiling or passing any pleasantry other than a nodding hello. Tyler was a different person altogether around him, quiet and deferential. Though I think this was based not so much on fear, just sober tradition, never questioned and never discussed.

Tyler was very much his mother's son – her only child. Miss Sis dotted on him, as might be expected, though I think she made a conscious effort not to smother him. Tyler seemed to both crave and despise this attention. Sometimes he could be quite cruel to her.

Miss Sis poured out three glasses of lemonade from a large pitcher, and laid a plate of sugar cookies on the kitchen table. The lemonade was freshly squeezed and ice cold.

'Tyler had you out looking at those snakes?' She inquired.

'Yes mam,' Rankin answered.

I found it difficult to even look up into her face – the image on the photo card still floating in my vision.

'I never go near that shed unless I have to. All that hissing and rattling. I've hated snakes since I was little girl. I found one coiled once behind the feed bucket in our barn. Roy, our handy man, killed it. Said it was a milk snake and had probably been drinking the cows dry at night. But then Tyler'd say that's an old wives' tale.'

Tyler snorted in annoyance.

'Probably *was* a milk snake and you'd been dumb to kill it. Bet after that ya'll were overrun with mice.'

She ignored the comment and reached over to pinch his ear.

'Tyler just hates it when I tell my little snake story. See he wants to be a scientist and go around the world just catching snakes.'

'A herpetologist, and they already know that.'

'I keep telling him that he'll never find a girl that'll marry a snake catcher. Not a nice girl like his momma.'

'What a shame. Can we go now?'

'Just hold on son. Let these boys finish their lemonade.'

Miss Sis then refilled both our glasses and smiled sweetly.

'So ya'll livin over there with that colored maid?'

'Yes mam,' said Rankin. 'Her name's Ophelia.'

'What a pretty name. So does Ophelia take good care of ya'll?'

'Oh, yes mam. Ever since we were little.'

'Well that's fine. You tell her to pay me a visit if she needs anything at all.'

'Thank you. I will.'

'Tyler tells me that your daddy works in the city.'

'Yes mam, he's in the oil business.'

'Really. You know now I've often wondered if there might be some oil out underneath our pasture. That back swamp is just so smelly. Full of gas. Maybe your daddy should have a look. Does he drill oil wells?'

'No mam. He just tells them where to drill.'

'Well I'm sure that's just as important. Certainly is a

lovely farm ya'll have. I mean just for the summer and weekends.'

Rankin smiled and gulped his lemonade.

'There must be a lot of work around there for just one maid and two boys?'

'Not too much. Ophelia has a vegetable patch. '

'She's growing strawberries and watermelons,' I added.

'How clever.'

'Then we also have the pig,' said Rankin.

'Tyler was telling me – a real fatty.'

'My father also plans to get some cattle when the fences are mended. Mr. Reives is supposed to be helping us. But he never shows up on the Saturday mornings my father's here. Says he's not well.'

'Mr. Reives suffers most mornings as far as we can tell.'

'Yesterday, he killed a rabbit in his backyard,' I said. 'Right in front of us.'

'Why that's terrible,' cooed Miss Sis.

'He told us to bring it home. But Ophelia made Rankin bury it out in the woods.'

'I can hardly blame her.'

'His daughter Alice was there too. Does she really play with dolls?'

'Now who told you that?'

Miss Sis narrowed her eyes and glanced over at Tyler.

'Alice makes dolls as a hobby – like some boys keep snakes. She's very good at sewing. Just last Christmas, Bryson's over in Folsom bought a whole box full of dolls from Gilbert Reives. Said he was clearing out the house. Mr Bryson sold out of them in a week. I bought one for Tyler's little cousin – a rag doll dressed up in a bonnet like an old-fashioned country lady. Just precious.'

'Can we go now?' Tyler snapped.

'Certainly son. Sorry to have been such a bore.'

She then winked at Rankin and me. Tyler waited at the door while we thanked her for the lemonade and cookies.

'Come see me again,' she called from the kitchen window.·.
'But just please don't go catching him any more snakes.'

Over the next weeks we saw a lot of Tyler. Nearly every morning he would appear in our bedroom at the crack of dawn.

'Rise and shine. Rise and shine,' he'd call out in his Gomer Pyle voice.

Ophelia began to set an extra place at breakfast as a matter of course. Tyler's reason for arriving so early was to 'supervise personally' Traveller's morning feed. He and Rankin had begun their campaign to fatten and groom the pig for the Parish Fair. They took the project very seriously.

Each afternoon for a week we'd visited selected house-holds in Buck Falaya to ask for donations of either money or kitchen scraps. Tyler worked out a sales pitch based on one he had used to push subscriptions for the Folsom Banner. First he would arrange us at the front door in descending order of height. Then he'd ring the bell – which was usually answered by a farmer's wife who knew him perfectly well.

'Hello there, Tyler.'

But this familiarity seemed almost to annoy him. He would launch into his pitch with grim formality.

'Good afternoon Mrs. Wilson. We would like involve you in an important civic project. My friends here . . . (pause and gesture) . . . have only recently moved to our community. They own a very large pig. We have formed a partnership and plan to enter this pig in the St. Tammany Parish Fair. We hope to bring back with pride to Buck Falaya the blue ribbon. So what can *you* do to help? My partner Rankin Calhoun will explain our needs.'

Rankin would then fumble and forget his lines.

'Well, we need slop – I mean table scraps – to fatten him up – the pig – cause he's . . . still underweight and lean for his age . . .'

Tyler, not wanting honesty to undercut the argument, would quickly cut in:

'. . . only a matter of a little extra feeding. All we ask is your unwanted kitchen scraps, or any other offer of help towards this goal. And what would you receive? Well, ours and the community's thanks. Your name would also be added to a list of honor to be posted above our hog pen at the livestock barn.'

The pitch seemed to work. Rankin and Tyler negotiated a steady supply of slop adequate for five Travellers. Each evening Rankin and I would set out after dinner with three feed buckets. Tyler would meet us at his road end and we'd collect kitchen scraps from about a half dozen houses. Often all three buckets would be full before we reached the last door. We'd then lug them back to the sleeping porch where Rankin would sort through the takings wearing a pair of rubber dishwashing gloves.

Some of the households made little or no effort to separate edible scraps from other trash. Rankin would pick out chicken bones, banana peels, egg shells, cigarette butts, beer tops – once even a tampax which sent Tyler howling across the yard. But we could hardly complain.

Traveller had to be kept in his pen during this operation in case he tore through the porch screen. He would stand with his forehocks hooked over the fence rail, his snout held high savoring the aroma that drifted across the yard.

The rich feedings increased his bulk week by week, almost day by day. The fatter the pig grew, the more sedentary and lethargic he became. During the hottest days of the summer he took to lounging in a dusty wallow underneath the front porch.

But to anyone with an eye for hogs it was apparent that Traveller was developing into a fine specimen. He possessed a symmetry and compactness of form – a square spring of rib and broad flat back uniform from shoulders to hams. His jowls were full but firm, with barely a wrinkle. His coat gleamed, and was taut and smooth to the touch. Best of all he carried this bulk with ease and self-possession – with a certain nobility.

Rankin was confident that Traveller was champion material, and perhaps even Judge Taylor would not have disagreed. But my brother was to end up disappointed in this respect, and in certain others.

Chapter 8

Tuesdays, twice-monthly in summer, Buck Falaya was visited by the St Tammany Parish Library Rural Extension Service – otherwise known as the 'book mobile'. This modified Winnebago van travelled a circuit of the outlying communities around Covington, lending out warped children's picture books, yellowed dime westerns and romances, and classics such as *The Last of the Mohicans* or *Jane Eyre*. It was a godsend as far as Rankin and I were concerned, for the farm had no TV.

The book mobile arrived around three in the afternoon and would sit for an hour in the gravel lot adjacent to Marslan's. The driver was a restless, brooding black man named Melvin, who spent most of his time leaning on the front fender, chain-smoking Camel cigarettes. Occasionally he'd climb up into the cab to listen to the radio.

Inside the cramped van the air was always stifling. The books lining the walls were held secure in their shelves in transit by detachable brass screens. Either one of two librarians accompanied the van to Buck Falaya – a Mrs Lott or a Mrs Thomas. Their names were embossed on interchangable plates which slotted into a plaque bolted to the desk.

'Everything's bolted down in the book mobile,' Tyler would say, 'except the books.'

Mrs Lott was the older of the two librarians, a handsome white-haired lady who was always helpful and gracious despite looking on the verge of heat collapse. She dressed in light flowery frocks, as though on a summer picnic, and forever clutched a white cotton handkerchief with which she'd dab the sodden edges of her make-up. On the days Mrs. Lott came I was allowed to browse the full hour until the children's table was littered with picture books.

Mrs Thomas – the other librarian – was not so tolerant. She was a sour-faced young woman with long thin brown hair and pale unhealthy skin. A thick pair of reading glasses clung to the end of her broad nose and at a certain angle would magnify her eyes, enhancing the overall impression of high indignation. Mrs Thomas took little pains to hide the fact that she detested this part of her job – summertime jaunts to please a handful of ignorant yokels. Her attitude was superior and dismissive, enough to put anyone off the idea of reading entirely.

It was a Mrs-Thomas-Tuesday when Ophelia and I gathered together a stack of books that had been checked out from the library over the last few weeks and had now fallen overdue. Rankin had gone off with Tyler to the river, and Ophelia was annoyed at the prospect of having to face Mrs Thomas to pay his fines. We reached Marslan's a few minutes before the book mobile was about to leave. Melvin was fitting the brass screens across the shelves, and Mrs Thomas had just locked her desk drawer.

'I'm sorry. We're closed,' she said without looking up from her card file.

Ophelia laid the stack of books on the desk.

'Well it's not three yet, and these books are overdue.'

Mrs Thomas snorted in annoyance and reopened the drawer to retrieve the strong-box. She then flipped quickly through the books.

'Some of these have been out for nearly a month,' she muttered to herself, as though speaking to us was a waste of breath.

Ophelia paid the fine without comment and pulled me away from the children's shelves. It was just at that moment that Alice Reives rushed through the door, thrusting a book out to Mrs Thomas as though it were a bus ticket.

'I'm sorry to be late,' she said, out of breath.

Mrs Thomas turned the lock in her desk with one hand and pointed to the wall clock with the other.

'The library is definitely closed.'

'But I've got a book to return.'

'Well it's now overdue. So you'll either have to return it to the main library in town and pay the fine there, or wait until next visit and pay Mrs. Lott.'

'But I've finished it.'

Her voice was barely above a whisper. She hesitated, and then laid the book on the desk.

'I'm so stupid. See, this is only volume one. I thought it was the whole novel.'

Mrs Thomas took a deep breath, and gazed up at the ceiling as though seeking patience.

'Then I suppose you will have to return *that* book to the main library, pay your fine and check out the second volume. Either that or try to be more on time.'

'But I hardly ever get to town. And I don't have anything else to read.'

Alice looked to us in an appeal for reason.

'Well, that's not my fault, dear.'

'I can see it right there on the shelf,' said Alice, 'volume two. Why can't I just take it?'

Mrs Thomas leaned forward on the desk and jangled her keys.

'Listen. You folks out here have to realise that we have rules that can't just be broken for your convenience. You already have the books brought right to your doorstep, and yet you still can't follow even the simplest requirement. Ya'll seem to think this is some sort of right. Well it's not. It's a privilege, and you can't just abuse it when you feel so inclined. Now the library is closed. Please leave.'

Alice Reives picked up the book on the desk and left without another word. Ophelia pushed me out of the van and turned to Mrs Thomas.

'So kind.'

Then, still clutching my arm, she rushed to catch Alice who was walking quickly up the road.

'Miss Reives?'

Alice turned in surprise. Her eyes were moist and swollen. She wiped her nose with the back of her hand.

'I'm sorry. Sometimes I can be so stupid.'

'Don't you worry, honey. That woman must have had crab apples for breakfast.'

Ophelia offered a Kleenex from her purse. Alice looked down at the tissue in the brown hand and hesitated – just a fraction of second. Then she glanced up with embarassment and took the tissue, blowing her nose. Ophelia pretended not to notice.

'What I wanted to say to you is that down at Mr Calhoun's farm there's a big box full old books from the house in New Orleans. I packed them up to read over the summer. You're welcome to come over and have a look. See if there's any you'd like to borrow. I won't even charge a fine if they're late.'

Alice smiled nervously and gazed up the road toward her mailbox and then back down to Marslan's.

'Thank you,' she said. 'But I don't want to be a bother.'

'No bother to me. I only read them one at a time.'
'Well maybe I could have just a quick look.'

Alice spoke hardly a word as we walked back to the farm –
not that she had much chance with Ophelia chatting away
about the hot weather, the lack of rain and her fear for her
tomatoes. Back at the house Ophelia sat Alice on the porch
and brought out a large cardboard box. It contained an odd
assortment of books, as Ophelia's reading habits could be
quite haphazard. She would pull anything down from the
shelf that caught her imagination – from James Michener
and Frances Parkinson Keyes to copies of my grandfather's
leather-bound Harvard classics, *The Canterbury Tales* or
Gulliver's Travels.

Ophelia made a pitcher of iced tea, and we sat watching
Alice sort intently through the contents of the box.

'I just can't decide on one.'

'Take a stack then,' said Ophelia.

'Oh no. I couldn't.'

'Why not. You think I'll manage to read all those books
in one summer? Makes my head spin. Borrow as many as
you like.'

But this seemed only to trigger another bout of indecision.
Alice stared down at the books, running her fingers across
the spines.

'Maybe I'll just take two for now. If you don't mind.'

'Fine with me.' said Ophelia. 'Come back for two more
when those are finished.'

Never once during the visit did Alice mention her father
or the day we first met in her backyard. An hour later she
thanked Ophelia and went away with two novels under her
arm, one of which I believe was *Dinner at Antoine's*. The
next afternoon Ophelia took us shopping in Covington, and
on our return she found a warm pan of blackberry cobbler,
wrapped in linen cloth, sitting on the kitchen window sill.

Alice visited the house a number of times over the next few weeks, either returning books or bringing cup-cakes and pralines which she'd bake for Rankin and me. Ophelia would serve coffee or iced tea and they would sit out on the porch and chat for an hour or so. Ophelia had at first found these visits somewhat tiring, as Alice often said little. But over time their conversation grew more relaxed and less one-sided.

Alice had lived all her nineteen years in Buck Falaya. Her mother had died when Alice was twelve, of a cancer that first appeared in one of her breasts and eventually spread to the bone. Ever since then Alice had cooked and kept house for Gilbert Reives, yet she rarely spoke of her father to Ophelia.

Mostly she talked about her days at Covington High School where she had graduated in the top five of her class. Her English teacher had encouraged her to apply to a teaching college in Pineville, Louisiana, but Alice had felt obligated to stay on with her father – or at least that was the excuse. She now spent all her time in Buck Falaya except for two weeks at Easter when she visited her mother's sister in Vicksburg, Mississippi. To afford the bus fair she took in sewing from local women – and then there were the dolls.

One afternoon Alice brought some samples of her hobby to show Ophelia: two neatly sewn rag dolls. One was a farmer with a floppy felt hat and red overalls; the other his wife in a long corn-flower print dress with a white shawl and bonnet. I remember not liking them much, the expressions on their finely stiched faces: pinched mouths and large almond eyes gazing sidelong as though expecting someone to sneak up from behind. But Ophelia made a great fuss over them.

Soon Alice began to visit Ophelia almost daily. Traveller would lounge in the dirt in front of the porch, lulled by the sound of their voices. Some afternoons I'd rouse him to show Alice a few tricks. The pig now weighed close to 300lbs, and yet would still sink onto his massive haunches when I commanded 'sit', or trot away with a heavy groan to retrieve an old tennis shoe. Alice would laugh and applaud at these performances.

No doubt her visits to the house would have continued through August had it not been for an incident that put an end to them altogether. To a small degree I was to blame for this – though completely by accident.

Tyler Fendleson was my sole friend that first summer in Buck Falaya – not counting Rankin. Yet it was only natural that he and my brother should become closer, being just a year apart in age. This didn't bother me too much. Sometimes I enjoyed spending the afternoon alone on the porch reading a book, or playing army or superheros out in the yard. These games were much too childish for Rankin – though Tyler was not above tossing the odd imaginary handgrenade which would explode in a shower of spit.

Probably the only time I felt truly left out was when one evening over dinner Rankin asked Ophelia if he and Tyler could go camping at the river – without me. I was almost in tears.

'Why can't I go?'

'Because you'd just get scared and want to come home in the middle of the night,' said Rankin.

'No I wouldn't. I've slept out before with the Cub Scouts.'

'That's not camping. Pitching tents in somebody's back-yard with a load of bedwetters.'

Ophelia reached over and slapped his hand.

'That's enough.'

'You can't stop me coming?' I shouted.

'Wanta bet.'

Ophelia held up both hands.

'Ain't nobody going nowhere if I hear any more arguing.'

Though she usually took my side in most arguments, Ophelia was oddly noncommittal on this point.

Rankin refused to give way no matter how I pleaded. This

left me utterly despondent. I wondered how they could have so little faith in me. What had I done or not done? I agonized over the possible reasons and eventually could lay the blame on one thing only – the rope swing.

That damn rope had become a fearful obsession with me. Nearly a dozen times I had climbed up and clung to the tree, unable to let go. Rankin now refused to even let me have a turn.

But the evening he first mentioned the campout I vowed to myself to make the jump. Long past bedtime I lay awake going through mental dry runs, clutching the knot between my thighs and stepping off the platform, letting go at the exact moment so as to drop straight into the pool.

Later that night I had a dream in which I leapt onto the swing, fearless, and sailed out over the water, up into the trees and straight into the sky like a Fourth of July rocket. I could see all of Buck Falaya below me, and the river winding away through distant fields.

The next morning I awoke feeling jittery and slightly sick. I couldn't finish my breakfast. Ophelia scraped the soggy cereal into Traveller's bucket.

'Something wrong with you?'

'Cherrios make me sick.'

Ophelia frowned in disbelief. But I didn't want Rankin to know my intention that day. He sat oblivious, spooning the last of the milk from his cereal bowl as he pored over a new comic book.

Tyler didn't show up until later that morning, and it wasn't until after lunch that we went down to the river. It was a hot, humid day, threatening with thunderstorms. I stood on the bank and watched Rankin go first on the swing, howling as he plunged into the cold water. My stomach grew tight as a fist. Tyler took his turn, and the rope swung back over the bank into my hands. I threw it over my shoulder and began to climb the wooden steps up the tree.

'Here we go again,' said Rankin.

He then swam over beneath the bank expecting to catch the rope when I dropped it. Reaching the last step, I hugged the broad trunk and inched around to the platform, my muscles in state of near tetany. I pulled the rope between my legs. Rankin called out:

'You got sixty seconds this time.'

He then began to count in a bland voice. I gazed out over the drop. All the carefully worked-out technique, the ruses to make myself jump, vanished in a seizure of panic. Rankin reached the count of sixty.

'You can drop the rope now.'

But I just stood there unable to move. Rankin shouted:

'Drop it, Milo.'

He then started up the bank, toward the tree. A sudden rush of adrenalin punched through my body, and I reached out with both hands and grabbed the rope. For one sickening instant I teetered on the edge of the platform and then lost my balance, falling backwards in a twisting motion. I spun down over the bank, still clutching the rope, unable to pull the knot back between my legs. The branch groaned and my hands began to slip as I sailed out across the river. I rose high over the surface and could hear Tyler scream:

'Let go.'

But there seemed no time to decide; in an instant I was hurtling back toward the tree. It was then that I released the rope and tumbled across the surface of the water, slamming into the tangle of hard oak roots that grew beneath the bank. A whine like the sound of dead airtime on TV filled my ears, and I slid under the surface of the river unable to breath.

I then remember hands reaching under my shoulders and lifting me out of the water. Rankin dragged me up into the dry sand. I gasped for air. Tyler shouted:

'Turn him over. He's got the wind knocked out of him.'

But when Rankin pushed me onto my side I screamed in agony.

'Jesus, I think his arm's broke,' said Tyler.

The only way home was by foot. Rankin put his arm around my shoulder and walked me up the path. My forearm had already begun to throb and swell. Blood from a gash in my chin dripped onto the toes of my sneakers. Another trickle ran down from a cut on my ankle. Rankin muttered over and over:

'I'm sorry, David. I didn't know it was your arm.'

Tyler had run ahead across the field, and by the time we reached the house Ophelia already had the car started. Alice Reives stood nervously at the passenger door. Ophelia knelt down and took my arm gently in her hands.

'What you done now?'

She then turned to Alice.

'Think it's broken. Can you sit with him on the way?'

'Certainly.'

Alice helped me into the back seat, and lay my head down in her lap. Rankin and Tyler climbed in beside Ophelia. The gravel road was rough and bumpy, and each time the car pitched Tyler would peek over the seat with a pained look. Alice smoothed the hair back from my forehead, and I closed my eyes and tried not to think about the pain in my arm. I then heard Rankin murmur:

'It was all my fault. I teased him into doing it.'

'Hush up now,' said Ophelia. 'Ain't nobody's fault. Things just happen.'

I left St Tammany Parish Hospital with my arm in a heavy plaster cast that had already begun to itch. By that time I was getting over the trauma and actually beginning to feel quite special. Ophelia had asked the emergency room doctor – a colossal man with curly brown hair and large soft hands – whether the break would heal properly.

'Honey,' he said, 'at that age, you get two ends of a bone in the same room and they'll mend.'

Ophelia stopped at Badeaux's Malt Shop on the way

home and bought us all ice-cream cones. A dark purple thundercloud appeared on the horizon as we drove north up the Folsom Highway. Twin bolts of lightning struck the forest a few miles ahead with a loud boom. The wind rose, showering the asphalt with dead pine needles. Just as we reached the Buck Falaya turnoff the clouds opened. Ophelia peered through the windshield, the wipers inadequate to handle such a heavy downpour. Water from the ditches flooded across the road and the river flowed rusty brown with the runoff. It was still raining heavily when we let Tyler off at his roadend.

'Maybe I should just get out here too,' said Alice.

'In this rain!' said Ophelia. 'Not on your life. Besides we drive right past your house.'

Ophelia pulled the car up in front of the Reives' gate.

'Come by tomorrow and see how the patient's doing.'

'You can sign my cast,' I said.

Alice smiled and thanked Ophelia again for the ice cream.

Just then I heard the gate slam and spotted Gilbert Reives making his way through the rain to the car. He marched up to the driver's side and pounded loudly on the roof. Ophelia rolled down the window, and he peered through at Alice.

'Just what the hell do you think you're doing?'

He wore no hat. The rain flowed in tiny rivulets over his thin dark hair and down his face.

'Am I dreaming or have you been out joy-riding with this girl – in the front seat. My dinner waiting too.'

'No.'

'No?'

He slammed his fist on the side of the door.

'Get the hell out of that car.'

Alice climbed out the passenger side. Gilbert walked around the front of the Buick and grabbed her arm tightly. He was shouting – though we couldn't hear what over the sound of the rain. Alice began to cry and tried to pull away.

'That's enough,' Ophelia muttered, and jammed the horn.

Gilbert swung about with a look of disbelieving fury. He then whispered something to Alice and let her go. She ran through the gate and into the house. Walking around to the driver's window he began to grin. But Ophelia spoke first:

'Nobody was out joy-riding. Can't you see this boy's broken his arm. I asked her to come along and help keep him still.'

Reives leaned through the window.

'Did I speak to you?'

The car was flooded with the smell of stale whiskey.

'Cause otherwise, you don't speak to me girl 'less you spoken to.'

Ophelia put the car in drive and took a deep breath.

'Mister, I speak to whomever I like, whenever I like.'

She then cranked the window up with a violent flourish and jammed the accelerator. Reives jumped back out of the way as the Buick lurched across the cattle guard.

Next morning Ophelia found four of my grandfather's novels stacked carelessly on the bottom step of the front porch. Alice never visited the house again.

Chapter 9

My father developed a keen obsession with fences that first summer at the farm. He was impatient to pasture some cattle before the Fall. Unfortunately, old Mr. Barton had not been much bothered about enclosed spaces. Large sections of fencing had been allowed to simply topple over, and of those posts still standing, most were rotten.

Working long hot Saturdays every weekend that June, George had managed to repair only a few hundred yards. He did this mostly single-handed, as Gilbert Reives claimed to suffer from 'floating vertebra' and rarely turned up. My father had begun to find the man somewhat less amusing.

Seeing no end in sight he decided to take on Joe Dreux to help. A number of farmers and landowners in the area employed Joe for occasional work, including the Fendlesons. His old beat-up Ford truck was a regular feature of Buck Falaya, though he lived alone in a trailer home about five miles north on a large tract of land owned by Chappapela

Lumber, who also employed him as caretaker. The first day on the job Joe arrived an hour after dawn and by dinner time he and my father had strung more fence than in the entire month previous. He was a strong, capable man, though at least twenty years George's senior.

Joe and my father were out working in the field that same Saturday morning when Tyler struggled into our backyard dragging a heavy burlap sack containing an old army surplus tent for the camp-out. It was set for that Monday night and Tyler wanted to try the tent out in the yard before lugging it all the way down to the river.

By breaking my arm I had indirectly achieved one end – Rankin felt so bad over the accident that allowing me along on the camp-out seemed small recompense. Ophelia was dead set against the idea. But my father had over-ruled her the night before at dinner.

'David'll be all right as long as it doesn't rain.'

Ophelia didn't argue the point. She had already described in detail what happened at the hospital and then the incident with Gilbert Reives. But George hadn't seemed overly disturbed.

'Better not to get involved in these things. Gil's just got a few backwoods attitudes.'

Ophelia snorted in general displeasure and then cleared the table without a word.

All that morning Tyler and Rankin argued over how best to pitch the tent. The sack was a tangled mess of guy ropes and stakes and steel poles of various lengths, along with a bundle of mouldy canvas. A certain Uncle Melton in Tickfaw had last used the tent on a rainy deer-hunting foray across the Mississippi border. The instructions had been lost. But Tyler claimed to know them by heart and tended to bridle at any doubt of his outdoor ability.

'I'm the country boy around here,' he kept saying.

To which Rankin finally replied:

'Then all we need is a country girl to put up the tent.'

This bickering went on until noon, when my father and Joe came up from the field for lunch. Ophelia brought out a large pitcher of iced tea and a po'boy for Joe, who sat out back in the grass under a shade oak. He ate his sandwich and watched Tyler and Rankin struggle with the sad, lopsided structure they'd managed to erect, the canvas sagging over the frame like the hide on a glue-house nag.

Eventually Joe stood up and finished off his tea in one long swallow. He brushed the crumbs off his trousers and strolled over to the tent. A half dozen or so steel poles lay unused in the grass.

'What you got here?'

'Them's extra,' Tyler snapped.

Joe tilted his hat back and wiped his forehead with a handkerchief.

'Got no extra poles with my tent. Maybe I's cheated.'

'So are you saying we put it up wrong?'

'I ain't saying nothing.'

Tyler cursed under his breath at the limp guy rope he was attempting to pull tight.

'Less of course you asking me.'

'Okay we're asking then.'

Joe had the tent back up within ten minutes – each pole in position, the canvas taunt and sturdy. It was much larger than I had expected, and smelled of wood smoke and old damp hunting boots. Joe tied back the front and rear flaps.

'Got to let it air out or else the canvas'll rot.'

He then sat down in the shaded open front of the tent and fanned himself with his hat.

'So you boys gonna sleep out here in the yard?'

'No way,' said Tyler. 'We're camping down at Jahnkee's bend.'

'By the river?'

'Yep.'

Joe raised his eyebrows.

'Never catch me sleeping down there. No sir.'

'Why not?'

'Best you don't know.'

'Know what?' Tyler scoffed.

'You ever slept in old forest?'

'Sure, I been camping lots, up at Money Hill and the scout camp at Avondale.'

'Ain't no old forest up there. That's all lumber company land – grown up in the last hundred years or so. Nearly all the woods 'round here be planted. What I'm talking about is old forest; never been cut. Just the same as it was a thousand years ago. Like down there by the river – that's old forest, probably the last of it in the parish.'

I remembered the trees along the trail to the rope swing, broad and twisted like wizened old men. Tyler smirked.

'What's so scary about some old trees?'

'Guess you never heard of the Billyjack.'

'What's a Billyjack?' Rankin asked.

'Come on, he's just trying to spook us,' said Tyler.

Joe looked over at the house, and then leaned back in the grass on one elbow.

'Now I'm only gonna tell ya'll this for your own good. This is the story how I heard it from my old grandpa. See one time long ago all round here was old forest – just one great big forest stretching all the way to Tennessee. Pine trees hundreds of feet tall, as broad as my truck. The Indians called it 'land of whisperin pines', cause whenever the wind blew it sounded like them big trees were passing secrets to each other. Funny things happened in that big old forest. Them dead Indians knew it. They prayed to the trees and the wind and the animals.'

'That's just stupid,' said Tyler.

'Maybe so, maybe not,' replied Joe.

'Anyway, one day a white man shows up in the forest. Come up from New Orleans which was just a little ol' river town then. He's a trapper – a low character, lives alone in a dirty old camp, sleeping on a bed of pine straw. It's a hard life, but he don't have it too bad. Plenty of deer and possum, lots of wild roots and other things to eat. He also has him a she-goat for milking. Keeps her outside the hut in a pen of woven pine saplings.

'So this trapper ain't wanting much in the way of basic necessities. The worst thing of all is the loneliness. He couldn't have no wife. It's too wild and rough. No woman'd stand for it. Sometimes he'd go for a year without even seeing a woman. The loneliness got worst in wintertime. Night'd fall and the north wind would whip up, and those pines'd start whispering secrets. That old trapper'd toss and turn in his cold bed till he couldn't stand it no more. So he'd creep out of his shack in the moonlight and snatch that she-goat out the pen and bring her in for a hug.'

'A goat?' Tyler sniffed.

'Yes sir. Next morning that trapper'd feel all dirty and sinful. He'd promise and pray never to do it again. But come nightfall he'd find hisself sneaking out again. Things went on like this a while till one day the trapper noticed something strange. The belly on that she-goat starts getting big. Trapper thought he was just imagining it. But a few weeks pass, and there's no mistaking. Soon that belly looks about to burst. The trapper starts getting nervous. Tells himself the she-goat must be sick. Decides it'd be best to put her out her misery. Maybe make her into a nice stew. But then the night before he's gonna do it there's a bad storm. The wind snaps off a big branch high up in one of them trees. It crashes down and breaks a hole in the pen. The she-goat gets loose.

'Next morning the trapper takes down his gun and sets out hunting for her. Picks up a set of tracks that lead straight into the forest. He follows the trail for hours. The further he goes, the deeper and darker that forest gets, until the trees are so tall and thick he can't even see the sky to tell the time. All the while he has this strange feeling, like something's watching him – something wicked. The trail gets harder to follow and soon the tracks just disappear. Night's falling by the time he decides to turn back home.

'First he's just walking regular-like. Then he gets that feeling again – something's watching. He walks faster but it's like he's being followed. Faster and faster, and then he starts to run. Soon he's crashing through the trees and the stickers – his clothes all torn, his arms bleeding. But he keeps running. Just when he thinks he might drop dead of fear and exhaustion the trapper breaks through into a clearing. Finds himself back in his old camp – just like a miracle. The sun's going down, and he runs straight into his hut. Climbs on his bed and holds the shotgun to the door all night. But nothing happens – not that night, the next or the one after.

'Weeks and months pass and the trapper goes back to his old ways. Laughs to think about how scared he got that day in the forest. Soon he forgets all about that she-goat.'

'Does she come back?' Rankin asked.

'Just wait and see. Now over the next years more people start moving into the forest. New Orleans is hungry for wood to build houses and river boats. That old trapper, he's smart. He stakes a claim on a big tract of land and begins cutting down the trees to sell for timber. Builds a big house and a saw mill where the old camp was and marries a fancy young bride from New Orleans. Towns are springing up all over the forest as more people move in to cut the trees and farm the bare land left by the lumbermen. That old trapper gets respectable. People start coming to him for advice; there's even talk of voting him to the state legislature. He starts wearing fine suits and a gold watch. Forgets how low he once lived. Forgets his old shack and his straw bed, and those giant trees now all sawed up into boards and planks though still whispering secrets whenever the wind blows.

'Then some strange things start to happen around the countryside. First it's nothing much. Tools going missing from the saw mills, clothes from washing lines, jewelry left

on bedside tables, kitchen knives. Folks just think it's thieves
come up from New Orleans. But then even worse things
begin to happen – horses let out their paddocks in the dead
of night and left to wander, laying hens found dead on the
roost – necks all twisted. Dead cats in wells. And there's these
odd tracks – like cloven hooves.

'Then one night something gets into the churchyard. Digs
up the shallow grave of an old colored slave. Scatters the
bones all over the place – and some them bones got teeth
marks where they been knawed on. Folks say it's just a stray
coyote or a mad dog. But they still can't explain them tracks
all over the churchyard.

'But of all the plantations in the area it's the old trapper's
that catches it worst. Every morning there's broken windows
and fences torn down. His well's fouled and his hunting dogs
poisoned with toadstools. One of his slaves nearly gets killed
when the drive-belt on the sawmill just snaps; finds it'd been
cut clean through. Then one night the mill just catches fire
and burns right to the ground. Pretty soon the trapper ain't
got much left except his land, that house, his wife – and his
new baby son.

'Now this child is his greatest treasure. Each evening the
trapper looks in on the nursery and says, 'Someday this bad
luck is gonna pass, and this house and all the land'll be yours.
You'll be the richest man in the Parish.

'But then one night something happens, something terrible. The trapper and his wife been sitting by the fire. Just
before bedtime his wife gets up from her chair and says she's
gonna check on the baby. Climbs up the stairs and suddenly
there's a horrible scream. The trapper leaps up the steps,
three at a time, and throws open the nursery door. Inside
his wife is laid out on the floor in a faint. There by the crib –
clutching a pillow in its nasty little hands – is the Billyjack.
Half goat, with a goat's body and four sharp hooves; the other
half, the top half, an evil-looking little man, thin and leathery
with a pinched-up face and a long scraggy beard. Eyes pink

and empty like glass marbles cause the Billyjack got no soul, just a tiny black heart full of hatred. The trapper screams in rage and charges across the room. But that old Billyjack just grins and disappears out the window with a clack of his hooves. Down in the crib the baby is as cold and blue as a drowned sailor. There ain't nothing the trapper can do. They bury the boy in a tiny coffin, and mark the grave with a weeping angel carved out of stone. It's still there today'.

'Did the Billyjack come back?' Rankin asked.

'Every night. Knocking at the trapper's door, tapping on the windows, banging an old tin pan out in the yard to keep the house awake. Eventually all the slaves run off. Then one day the wife just packs up and leaves, goes back to New Orleans. The trapper's all alone again, and he takes to drinking. Lets the house fall into a ramshackle state. But still the Billyjack torments him, even gets so bold as to sneak into the house when the trapper's too drunk to notice. Wanders from room to room, tearing up the furniture, fouling the carpets. One night the trapper decides he's had enough. He loads his shotgun and waits in the old nursery until there's the light clip, clip of the hooves up the steps. Neighbors that night heard an almighty racket – gunshots and glass breaking and shouts and curses. Then everything goes silent. Next morning they find the trapper at the bottom of the stairs, his neck broke.

'They buried him in the graveyard next to his baby son. Put a big stone slab over the grave – to keep the animals out. A hunting party went out tracking the Billyjack but found nothing. A few nights later the house caught fire and burned to the ground. Over the years the property grew over with weeds and young pines. Today you'd never know there was even a house there'.

'So what happened to the Billyjack?' Tyler asked, with a little less bravado.

'Some people say he went straight to hell. But others believe he's still living out there in the old forest, or what's left of it. Still making mischief. Can't say which I believe. But then I did hear one last thing. Years later there was a preacher's wife who always made a point of laying flowers on the forgotten graves in the cemetery. None was more forgotten than that trapper's. But every time she laid flowers on his grave, next day she'd find them torn and scattered over the grass. Then one morning she noticed deep cuts in the stone grave slab, like something been scratching and pawing at it for years. Today nobody ever visits that old cemetery.'

By that time my father had wandered up from the barn. Joe put on his hat and called out:

'Bout ready to hit it again, Mr Calhoun?'

'Unless you do a good rain dance.'

'Passin, passin.'

Joe chuckled and winked at us.

'Ya'll keep an eye out now.'

He then strolled over to my father and the two of them set off across the hot dusty field, back to their fence posts.

Chapter 10

Joe Dreux had not exactly fired my enthusiasm for camping. In fact, I began to regret ever having been so determined. Rankin and Tyler debated at length the possible existence of a Billyjack. Tyler argued that it was just a tall tale.

'Sure he could've done it to a goat. But nothin'd happen. You ever seen a cat that barks, or a cow in the Kentucky Derby.'

'Maybe it's never been tried before.'

'Don't be stupid. Besides if all this happened so long ago it'd be dead by now.'

'Could be a ghost.'

This went on until, to my horror, they began to dare each other to go Billyjack-hunting. Tyler was certain that Joe had been describing the old Lambs Road cemetery. Lambs Road was an overgrown dirt track that disappeared into the woods off Brewster Highway. They decided to go the night of the campout – not even having asked my opinion.

That Sunday before the campout I remember lying in bed with all the lights on, too afraid to sleep. I asked Rankin if he really thought there were such things as ghosts.

'You believe in God and Jesus, don't you?' He said.

'Of course.'

'Well if you believe in God the Father and God the Son, then you got to believe in the Holy Ghost. There's one spook for you.'

Rankin then rolled over and fell asleep. The logic of this seemed unassailable. Having no clear idea then (or now) just what the Holy Spirit was, I'd come to visualize it as a floating, moth-eaten sheet, swirling through the rafters at St Alban's. Surely this meant nothing was beyond the bounds of reality, no matter how terrifying.

Monday afternoon Ophelia seemed almost to read my thoughts. She was filling a cardboard box with provisions – Dixie cups and paper plates, Sunbeam Bread and cans of Dinty Moore Beef Stew.

'Rankin, I best not hear about you trying to frighten anybody.'

My brother was emptying all the icetrays from the freezer into a small cooler. He looked up and grinned at me.

'Milo says he's not afraid of anything.'

These were my words – said more than once.

'No matter. You mind me now.'

Tyler arrived later pushing a large, squeaky wheelbarrow heaped with gear. Ophelia came out on the porch and watched as Rankin tied our sleeping bags on to the sides. Just as we were about to leave she handed me a tray of fudge brownies to carry in my good hand. She then waved us off.

'You boys behave.'

Halfway across the field, I turned back toward the house and saw Ophelia still out on the porch. I wished for nothing more than to be there by her side.

The sun was still high and hot when we reached the edge of the woods. Rankin and Tyler raced ahead down the trail with the wheelbarrow, their voices fading through the trees. I gazed up into the green twilight of those massive pines, certain they were spreading the news of our presence.

By the time I reached the river the tent was already laid out on a flat patch of ground just above the bank. Tyler's transistor radio was perched on a tree branch, crackling out Conway Twitty on WARB. Once the tent was up and my sleeping bag unfurled inside I began to feel a little better.

Tyler brought out his boy scout hatchet to chop up twigs and branches for the fire. He kept this in a leather holster on his belt which also held a huge Bowie knife with a staghorn handle. This knife seemed to serve no useful purpose, though Tyler boasted that he could field-gut a deer in two minutes, should the need arise.

Near dusk the mosquitos started to bite, and Tyler and Rankin decided to go in the river. Neither had brought shorts so they peeled off their clothes on the bank and swam naked.

'Come on in, Milo,' Tyler called. 'Ain't nobody lookin.'

He stood in the shallows, his tiny, shrivelled fig of a prick tucked under that massive belly. I didn't find this particularly inviting. The most daring I could muster in the end was to strip down to my underpants and sit shivering in the water, the cast held over my head.

Rankin and Tyler later dried off by the fire and slipped back into their clothes. I climbed into the tent and peeled off my wet underpants. I had not thought to bring an extra pair, so I had to get dressed in trousers alone. I then found two long branches and stuck them in the sand by the fire to hang my underpants out to dry.

Rankin was mortified.

'I ain't looking at those stainy things all night, Milo.'

'It won't take that long.'

'Should of just skinny dipped,' said Tyler.

'Milo's too shy,' replied Rankin. He then pinched the tip of his pinky finger.

'See he's only got this little cuppy dick.'

I grabbed a handful of sand and threw it at him. Trying then to scramble out of his reach I kicked one of the drying branches and toppled my underpants into the fire.

'Get 'em out,' I screamed.

But Rankin and Tyler just danced around the flames in mock panic.

'Fire, fire.'

Rankin finally used a stick to fish them out – black and smoking, the elastic melted. He slung them far out into the river.

I watched in misery as they floated slowly downstream. Ophelia kept a strict reckoning of all our socks and underwear – nothing went unnoticed. For the next half hour or so I sat down on the river bank sulking. Rankin eventually said he was sorry, and that it was only a joke. Tyler was cooking a can of beef stew on the gas stove and I wandered back up to the camp site.

Night had fallen, and the light from the fire danced in and out of the shadow of the trees, and out across the surface of the river. Tyler lit his lantern and hung it from a tree branch. Hundreds of moths and tiny insects fluttered in spirals around the light, singeing their dusty wings on the hot glass. We almost had to shout over the sound of crickets.

Tyler ate most of the beef stew, along with half a box of Saltine crackers. Later he disappeared into the tent and returned with his Tom and Jerry pencil pouch. He was also carrying a can of Del monte String Beans.

'That for your dessert?' Rankin asked.

'Nope. You'll see.'

Tyler grinned and turned out the lantern. By the light of the fire he produced two completely unsmoked True Greens.

'Stole these special for tonight.'

He lit both cigarettes with a burning twig, and handed one to Rankin. He then leaned back on a piece of drift wood and blew a perfect smoke ring that drifted away into the darkness.

'Man this is great. All that's missing is the naked girls.'

Rankin laughed, and then choked on his cigarette.

'Like in those pictures?'

'Yea. Like the redhead. Hey, you ever seen a for-real naked girl?'

'No.'

'I seen my cousin once. But she's only eight so I guess it don't count. I mean I got bigger titties.'

Tyler stirred the fire with a stick.

'I seen somebody jerk off once.'

'When?'

'Last year at school. This guy named Ernie Ross – big and dumb. He'd failed sixth grade about three times. The only reason they passed him into seventh is cause he's bigger than most of the teachers. Anyway, one day a bunch a guys told Ernie they'd pay a dime each to see him jerk off behind the gym. So everyone follows him around the back. Ernie kneels down by the wall and pulls it out, starts wacking away. Must have been about twelve guys watching. Only took a couple minutes and this white stuff comes shooting out into the dirt. Looks kinda like spit. Everybody's screaming and pretending to puke. Old Ernie's trying to catch 'em to get his dimes. Then this retardo named Dean Demarko picks it up on a stick. Brings it out to the playground and throws it at some screaming fifth grade girls. Dean and Ernie got pulled out of class and suspended. I got a week's detention just for watching.'

Tyler grinned and then reached over and shoved the unopened can of green beans into the hot embers. Rankin scooted away from the fire.

'Are you nuts? That'll explode.'

Tyler seemed unconcerned.

'Don't worry. We do it all the time at Boyscouts.'

He poked at the can with his stick. Flames licked up the side of the label.

'I tried jerking off a couple of times,' said Tyler. 'It feels okay but ain't nothin happens. Have you ever come?'

'Well . . . sort of,' said Rankin.

'How can you sort-of come.'

'I did have this dream.'

'Was it with a girl.'

Rankin hesitated.

'Promise you won't ever tell anybody.'

'Sure I promise. Scout's honor.'

Tyler held up three fingers. Rankin turned to me.

'Go on down by the river, Milo.'

'Why?'

'Just do it or you'll never come camping with us again.'

So I got up reluctantly and sauntered down to the river's edge straining to hear what Rankin was whispering. A few minutes passed and Tyler suddenly broke into hysterical laughter. Rankin muttered:

'What's so funny.'

But Tyler could hardly breathe, much less speak. Looking up into the firelight I could see that Rankin was not even smiling. I had not heard a word of what was said, and wouldn't until at least two years later. It was only then that Tyler finally broke his promise to Rankin and told me the whole story.

In the dream Rankin described he was out in the backyard at Franklin Place washing Traveller. The blue plastic baby pool was full of warm suds and the pig grunted happily as he always did in the bath. Rankin had just started scouring Traveller's back when he happened to glance up at the house next door. Just above the Conroy's deck was a full-length window in which the curtains were pulled open. There, standing in the bright sunshine, was Mrs Conroy, fresh out the shower. She was drying herself with a small towel, rubbing it up and down her large sagging breasts.

Rankin watched in amazement as she made no signs of having noticed him below. The scrub brush dropped from his hand and his heart began to pound. A warm, almost nauseous feeling spread from the pit of his stomach. Reaching down to look for the brush under the suds he then felt something firm and realised that Traveller had developed a huge hard-on. He jerked his hand away and looked up at the window again. This time Mrs Conroy was staring straight into his eyes – making no move to cover herself. That's when Rankin awoke and found his pajamas moist and sticky.

Tyler's interpretation of this was strictly literal.

'Imagine having your first wet dream jerking off a pig.'

But this, as I said, was years later. That night at the campout Tyler could hardly speak, rolling back from the fire with that high girlish cackle. It was so infectious that I even began to laugh.

'Shut up, Milo,' Rankin shouted. 'You don't even know what's funny.'

Tyler finally managed to sit back up again.

'I'm really sorry,' he cried.

By then the green bean can had sprung a leak, and steam was whistling out across the embers like a blast furnace. Tyler giggled again and leaned over the fire, poking the can with a stick.

'What's happened to this thing?'

Just then the tin burst with a muffled pop, sending a shower
of sparks and steaming beans in all directions. I jumped down the bank shaking burning embers out of my hair and off my shirt. Looking back up to the fire I caught a glimpse of Tyler slapping at a string bean stuck to the side of his nose like some long green leech. Rankin was laughing so hard he could barely manage to relight the lantern.

The blast had all but extinguished the fire. Glowing coals were scattered over the sand. Tyler grinned as he raked the fire back together with his boot. His face was smeared with ash and a large red boil was forming across his nose.

'Told you it'd be neat. Never know when they'll blow.'

*

Rankin and Tyler later struck up a game of cards on the lid of the ice chest. I was feeling glum again. Embers from the explosion had left two dime-sized holes burned into the front of my shirt. Losing my underwear would have been crime enough for Ophelia; now I saw no hope of pardon.

A warm breeze picked up and stirred the trees. A silent flash of heat lightning lit the sky, though there was not a cloud in sight. Nothing more had been said about cemeteries and Billyjacks, and I took this as a good sign. I lay by the fire on my sleeping bag, drowsing to the sound of the crickets and the card game.

'Got any Queens?'

'Go Fish.'

'Got any sevens.'

'Nope, Go Fish.'

Just as I drifted off to sleep I heard Tyler ask in a low voice:

'How did your mother die anyway?'

'It was in an accident.'

'What kind of accident?'

'In a car.'

Tyler paused a moment.

'Sorry to ask. It's just that I can't imagine my momma dead.'

Rankin replied quietly, 'I can't imagine mine alive anymore.'

The next thing I can remember is being awoken by the glare of a flashlight shining down in my face.

'You coming or not, Milo?'

For an instant I forgot where I was and who could be talking to me.

'Coming where?'

'To Lambs Road,' said Rankin. 'Are you coming or staying?'

'Here by myself?'

'Maybe that Billyjack'd keep you company,' said Tyler.

'Make up your mind now,' Rankin snapped.

'Okay, just wait a minute.'

I unzipped the sleeping bag and pulled on my sneakers. Tyler had already set off up the trail with his lantern.

'What time is it?' I asked.

Rankin held the flashlight to his wrist.

'Just after one. Hurry up.'

He then turned and walked away, leaving me in the dark. I jumped up and tripped after him, keeping my eyes on the luminous Ked's tab at the back of his sneakers. The trail seemed unfamiliar in the dark, the trees looming up out of sight. My teeth began to chatter even though it was a warm night. Reaching the edge of the woods, Tyler extinguished the lantern so as not to attract attention. We then made our way across the pasture under a half moon. Not a word was spoken. Looking off into the distance I could see moonbeams reflected in the darkened windows of our house. I longed to be there in my room, in my bed, with Ophelia just down the hall.

We climbed over the creaking barbed wire fence at the far edge of the pasture. Charlie Brown began to bark off in the distance.

'Stupid mongrel,' Tyler whispered.

Buck Falaya was black and still as we walked down Brewster Highway, the only sound being the whine of over-night trucks rolling out along LA 7. At first we couldn't even find the entrance to Lambs Road. Tyler ran up and down the same stretch of pavement three or four times.

'I'm sure it's here.'

Finally Rankin shone his flashlight through an opening in the dense undergrowth. Tyler stood next to him and whispered:

'Guess I'll go first.'

He picked his way through the stickers and in among the trees. Rankin and I followed. A dozen or so paces down the track Tyler stopped to relight the Coleman. He pumped the primer and struck a kitchen match. The gas hissed and sputtered and the mantle burned brillant white. Our arms and legs cast gigantic shadows across the thick wall of briars and scrub oak that lined the track. We set off.

Deeper into the woods the trail grew narrow and cavern-ous, with the low overhanging branches blanketed in dead pine needles. Walking in that cramped pool of light I felt oddly confined; the woods seemed to close in behind us. All along I could not help imagining that something was following us in the copse just beyond the edge of the path.

Soon we came upon a toppled wooden fence post and a tangle of rusting barbed-wire.

'Come see the old well first,' Tyler whispered and led us off the track onto a narrow trail.

'Watch out where you step.'

He swept the lantern across the ground ahead until the light fell upon a large brick-lined pit choked with rotting branches. A frog leapt into the brown water and floated there, its eyes glistening.

'What's a well doing way out here?' Rankin asked.

'Beats me.'

Tyler kicked a pine cone into the water and the eyes dipped beneath the surface. He then moved off with the lantern.

'Not much further now.'

We walked a few hundred feet more up the track, or it might have been half a mile. Eventually we reached a tumbled-down wire fence. Tyler held the lantern high. Just at the edge of the light I could make out a dozen or so pale gravestones.

Rankin stepped over a broken wrought iron gate.

'See any hoofprints?' Tyler whispered.

'I can't see shit. Bring the light.'

Tyler reached for the Bowie knife in his belt and followed Rankin into the graveyard. The two of them wandered among the stones with the lantern, reading out the inscriptions, while I stayed by the gate. It wasn't as frightening a place as I had expected – more sad with accumulated neglect. No one had tended the graves for years. The ground was overgrown with weeds and sapling pines; the stones were tilted and broken either from subsidence or vandalism.

Tyler called out:

'Hey Milo, come take a look at this one.'

He and Rankin stood at a gravestone on the other side of the cemetery. I didn't have a flashlight so I made Tyler hold the lantern up to light my way over the uneven ground. Rankin was crouched beside a large marble gravestone edged with scrolls and angels. It was easily the finest in the cemetery and must have been expensive in its day. The inscription read:

'Elizabeth Clement, beloved wife and mother. Born 1831. Died 1857. A bower of sweet repose.'

Next to it was a another small stone, obviously a child's. It was carved in the same marble, but with the shape of an angel, the figure so worn it appeared almost to have melted.

Rankin pointed his flashlight at the marker.

'See what it says, Milo.'

So I bent down close to read the worn inscription. Just then Rankin switched off the flashlight and Tyler extinguished the lantern. The light from the mantle faded into blackness.

'That's not funny,' I said. 'Turn it back on.'

But there was no answer.

'I'll tell Ophelia.'

Again, only silence. I decided to wait them out. Minutes passed and the darkness began to seem like a tomb.

'Ya'll better not be leaving me here.'

But there was still no reply. I began to panic and holler:

'Rankin. I'll tell Ophelia. Rankin!'

Tyler struck a match only a few feet away.

'Keep it down.'

He relit the lantern.

'It was only a joke.'

Rankin grinned and I grabbed the flashlight from him and switched it on.

'Never do that again.'

But what happened next was not planned. I stepped back away from the gravestone and the grass underfoot suddenly gave way. My leg plunged into the ground up to the thigh and I fell backwards, the flashlight twirling into the air.

I struggled to pull my leg up but was unable to get any leverage. A horrific image passed through my mind in that instant – frail bony fingers reaching up to clasp my ankle.

'Get me out, get me out,' I wailed.

First Rankin grabbed my good arm and tugged backwards – but the angle was wrong. Then he and Tyler took hold of my leg and with one almighty heave wrenched it up out of the ground, leaving my sneaker buried under the grass. But I couldn't have cared less.

Tyler was already running toward the gate, the lantern swinging wildly. I raced passed him. Rankin called from behind:

'Ya'll wait.'

But we neither paused. Never in my life have I run so furiously – my heart pounding in my throat. I crashed down the track heedless as the sock on my shoeless foot bunched over my toes and eventually slipped off. Behind I could hear Tyler's footsteps, though in my panic I imagined the light clip of hooves.

It seemed only a few minutes before we burst out of the woods back onto the pavement. My bare foot was bleeding from the stickers. I began to limp up the road. Rankin dashed up beside me.

'Wait,' he whispered. 'Where are you going?'

'Home.'

'You can't. Ophelia'd murder us.'

But I wasn't listening. The moon was high and the road clearly lit.

'Come on David. It was probably just a rabbit hole. No big deal.'

I kept walking. Tyler and Rankin fell in behind me and began to whisper. We crossed over the cattle guard to the farm, and Rankin then grabbed my arm.

'Listen David. We'll go back to the campsite and build a big fire, play cards till morning.'

'Let me go,' I said.

Just then Tyler let out an odd whimper and pointed toward the house. Rankin looked around.

'What the hell?'

Moving through the trees toward us was a large white apparition. It seemed to glide over the ground like some huge pale fish. Tyler turned to run.

'Wait a second,' said Rankin.

We then heard a grunt.

'Dammit Traveller.'

The pig trotted up and sniffed at our hands, and then began to lick my bare foot. Rankin reached down and scratched behind his ears.

'That's the second time in a week he's gotten out.'

I took my chance then and ran toward the house.

'Stop!' Rankin hissed.

But I never looked back. Climbing the front porch, I caught a last glimpse of them leading the pig around the side of the house. I pounded on the door and waited for the light to appear in Ophelia's window.

Chapter 11

Not long after breakfast the next morning Rankin appeared, tired and filthy, on the back porch. Tyler loitered out in the yard in hope of pancakes and maple syrup. But Ophelia's sharp voice from the kitchen put paid to that notion, and he and his wheelbarrow squeaked away up the drive toward home.

It was to be the first and last campout of the summer. I had confessed all to Ophelia, omitting only the exact location of my lost shoe. I was afraid she'd make me go find it. There was no question then of my ever setting foot down Lambs Road again. Far as I know my sneaker is still rotting away down that hole.

Ophelia punished us for a week. We were not allowed to leave the yard. Rankin was so furious he wouldn't even look at me. Most days he spent on the front porch, thumbing restlessly through old comic books. But I was even further restricted having to wear my Sunday shoes in lieu of sneakers.

'I best not see even a scuff,' Ophelia had warned.

The days passed achingly slow. One morning Joe Dreux arrived at the house hauling a tractor mower on his trailer. I ran up the drive to meet him.

'See you survived the Billyjack,' he said, stepping out of the cab of his truck.

'That was just a story,' I replied.

He grinned and climbed up onto the trailer to loosen the guy ropes.

'Why isn't Mr Reives cutting the yard?' I asked.

'Couldn't tell you. Your daddy done asked me to mow it now.'

Joe hefted a gas can out the bed of the truck and emptied it into the tank of the tractor. He then fired the engine and backed the mower down off the trailer on two stiff planks of wood.

'Wanta ride?' He shouted.

I climbed up in the seat beside him and we pulled into the front yard, cutting the long grass in a circuit of ever-diminishing squares. Joe showed me how to control the throttle, and let me steer on the straight runs. On one circuit we swung wide to mow the narrow strip of grass on the other side of the drive near the front gate. Joe raised the cutting blades to cross the gravel and I looked up and saw Gilbert Reives standing at the cattle guard. Joe also saw him and tipped his hat. But Reives just glared at us, hands deep in his pockets.

Later I learned that my father – always the businessman – had that week sent Reives a formal letter severing their agreement over his work at the farm. Gilbert had not taken this well – and especially not when he saw Joe Dreux on that mower.

A few days later Tyler appeared at the house for a visit. Ophelia's anger had eased somewhat, and that afternoon she brought us ice cream out on the front porch. Tyler waited until she'd gone back into the house and then whispered to Rankin:

'They're saying around town that your daddy's a nigger-lover.'

'Why?'

'Hiring a colored over a white man.'

'You mean Joe Dreux.'

'Yep.'

'But Reives hadn't done any mowing for three weeks.'

'Don't matter.'

Now this was truly ironic, for as much as I'd like to credit my father, George Calhoun was no more a civil rights advocate than a lumberjack. Press him and my father would spout the same segregationist attitudes his father had held thirty years before. But on the other hand he didn't care much how a job was done, or by whom, as long as it was done properly. That went for anything from mowing the lawn to looking after his children.

Word spread around the area, mostly via Gil Reives I imagine, that my father was one of them New Orleans liberals (maybe even Jewish) come up to cause trouble in Buck Falaya. Tyler even heard one kid swear that Ophelia was really our mother, and we were all hiding out up here to keep George from being arrested for miscegenation. Tyler reported all this gleefully. Then he thanked Ophelia politely for the ice cream and headed off home for his dinner.

We didn't see Tyler again for a few days. That is, not until one afternoon when Ophelia finally relented and called an end to our confinement. Rankin and I wandered over to the Fendlesons. Charlie Brown announced our presence a quarter mile up the drive. Miss Sis stood waiting in the kitchen door as we walked into the yard.

'You boys seen Tyler?'

'No mam. Not today,' said Rankin.

'That's odd. It's been nearly two hours since I sent him up to Marslan's on my bicycle to pick up a few things.'

'Want us to go have a look.'

'Would you please? And tell that boy to get home now. I'm completely out of butter.'

Rankin and I made our way up the hot gravel track to the highway. Nearing the bridge we could tell something was up at Marslan's. A group of about fifteen kids had gathered out in front of the store – most of the childhood population of Buck Falaya. They loitered under the portico and in the gravel lot. Then I spotted Frank Bone sitting on his motorcycle under the trees across the road. A short, dumpy teenager from Talisheek, known to me only as Stewy, slouched against a fence post next to him, smoking a cigarette. They were talking to Alison Brewster, a thin, foul-mouthed local girl with hardened looks far beyond her fourteen years. Playing in the dirt at their feet was her grimy, tow-head little brother Floyd.

Alison caught sight of us first.

'Hey tootsie pops. Yo mammy know ya'll out?'

Stewy laughed loudly. Frank regarded us silently over his cigarette. I then noticed Miss Sis's bicycle, with its flowery wicker basket, parked in the rack outside. Alison shouted again:

'Tell turd-the-third we're all waitin out here.'

Rankin and I slipped inside the store. Tyler stood at the back by the magazine stand, paging through a copy of *Southern Living*. A bag full of groceries and a carton of Rex Rootbeer sat at his feet.

'Can you believe this?' He said. 'Boner sent in that hag to tell me he'll wait til the store shuts.'

'Just because of those pictures.'

'Guess so.'

'Then why don't you give em back.'

'Why should I? Finders keepers. Anyway, he'll just beat me up for having them in the first place.'

'Well you got to do something.'

'It's not four o'clock yet. Maybe they'll get bored.'

But Frank did not get bored. Just about a quarter to five Marslan looked at his watch and told us that he was about to close up. I suspect he even wanted to see what would happen. Tyler peered out the window.

'Guess I'll have to make a run for it.'

Frank was now in high spirits at the thought of Tyler's imminent murder. He and Stewy had begun to wrestle in the grass. Frank quickly won and was sitting on Stewy's chest when Tyler finally made his move. He burst out the screen door and tossed the groceries into the wicker basket. Grabbing the handlebars he dashed across the gravel and leapt into the seat. A cry arose from the assembled children. Bone turned and spotted his quarry pedaling frantically down the road.

At first the Honda wouldn't start. Frank bounced up and down on the kick pedal. But finally the engine caught, and he jammed his heel onto the gear shift and roared off with Stewy on the seat behind, the heels of his cowboy boots scraping over the asphalt.

Rankin and I chased down the street after them along with the rest of the mob. Ahead in the distance I could see three figures floating in the heat haze over the road. I imagined a scene out of some gangster movie: Stewy holding Tyler's arms back while Frank worked him over. But it was a much different scene we came upon.

The Honda lay in the middle of the road next to a pool of foaming brown liquid and shattered glass. Frank and Stewy had retreated to the ditch on the far side. Miss Sis's bicycle lay on the shoulder, its front wheel twisted, spokes bent and broken. Tyler stood astride it, brandishing a king-sized bottle of Rex Rootbeer like a club.

'Come on you bastards,' he screamed and launched the bottle at the Honda. It thudded against the gas tank and then shattered on the asphalt.

Frank started across the road, but Tyler pulled another Rex from the cardboard carton at his feet.

'I'll crack your dumb head open.'

Frank hesitated and then began to pace back and forth along the edge of the road.

'That kid's a nut case,' Stewy whined.

Rankin held up his hands and stepped over to pick up the bicycle while I gathered up most of the groceries. He then began to push it along the shoulder towards the Fendleson's road end – the broken spokes clattering over the front fork.

'Come on Tyler. Let's go now.'

Tyler backed away still clutching the rootbeer bottle, but Frank made no move to follow. He crouched over his motorcycle to inspect the damage. Then, pulling it upright, he shouted:

'You've had it, Fendleson.'

But the threat sounded somewhat lame under the circumstances.

Together we walked up the drive in silence. Tyler's face and ears were bright red, and there was a violent scowl on his face. Neither Rankin nor I dared speak to him. But once out of sight of the road, he began to laugh, a choked, breathless giggle. I couldn't tell if it was elation or hysteria. He danced up to the house with his rootbeer bottle, swiping at the azalea bushes.

August arrived, hot and airless, and I began to dread the passing days and the prospect of a return to New Orleans and St Francis Xavier. One morning a letter arrived for E. Rankin Calhoun from the St. Tammany Parish Fair Commission. It was to confirm Traveller's entry in the Junior Livestock Competition. Rankin was given a stall number and asked to arrive with Traveller at the livestock barn on August 21st at 7 am. Joe Dreux offered to take them in his trailer. The pig now weighed well over 300 lbs and was in prime condition for his age. Rankin and Tyler felt sure their entry would take a ribbon. And Traveller might just have managed it – had it not been for a watermelon.

Now this particular watermelon could probably have won its own ribbon had Ophelia bothered to enter it in the Fair. She had grown it in the vegetable patch out behind the house. That summer our kitchen overflowed with the fresh produce Ophelia cultivated in that small plot: snapbeans, okra, cucumbers, tomatoes, potatoes, cabbage, lettuce, spring onions – and a dozen or so plump watermelons.

To Reives these watermelons were a great joke. One morning, not long before my father fired him, Gilbert had wandered over to the edge of the plot to watch Ophelia and I dig weeds in the hot sun. He crouched down by the fence and ran his hand over the glossy rind of the largest.

'Now that's a real beauty. Looks like you plannin' a watermelon feast. You gonna save me a slice?'

Ophelia barely looked up from her garden trowel.

'Maybe if you'd done one stroke of work to help grow it.'

'That's not very neighborly. Bet you old Joe gets a big juicy slice.'

Ophelia smiled.

'He just might.'

'See now. I'd call that unfair. Favoritism. Thought you folk were all for equality. Guess not when it comes to watermelon.'

Ophelia ignored the comment and went back to her weeding. Reives spat once and wandered off. We rarely saw him again after my father's letter. On occasion Rankin and I would pass the house as he sat out on the porch with his bottle. Sometimes he'd yell things at us from his rocking chair – most of them incoherent. I suspect he was also drunk when he paid our farm the midnight visit that started all the trouble that August.

It had been a stifling hot day. The electric fans in the house were no better than useless – just stirring the heavy warm air. Ophelia allowed Rankin and I to pull our mattresses out onto the back sleeping porch. This was more my idea of camping out – falling asleep to the sound of the crickets and whippoorwills, a light evening breeze and no mosquitos.

The first time I was awoken that night was to the sound of heavy breathing in my ear. Rolling over on the mattress I found Traveller pressing his snout against the screen just beside my head. Once again he'd tripped the latch on his pen and was loose in the yard. Rankin moaned:

'Go on. Git!'

Traveller hesitated a moment and then turned and vanished into the dark. I fell instantly back asleep. It seemed only seconds later when I was awake again – bolt upright on the mattress, my heart pounding. Someone was out in the backyard, cursing furiously. I peered through the screen into the moonlight but could see nothing. The voice was gruff and out of breath, though familiar. Then the cursing stopped and all was silent. A moment later there was a wrenching screech.

Rankin jumped up from his mattress and threw open the screen door.

'Traveller!'

But the squeals quickly receded in the dark. He ran out across the yard toward the barn. The kitchen light flicked on. Ophelia came out onto the porch in her night gown, a flashlight in her hand.

'What the devil's going on?'

'Something's happened to Traveller.'

Ophelia went out onto the back stoop and swept the flashlight beam across the yard. Just beside the vegetable garden lay our champion watermelon, the rind cracked and broken in the dirt. Nearby the grass was smeared with blood and mucus. Ophelia switched off the flashlight when Rankin returned.

'We have to go find him.'

'Not tonight.'

'But he sounded bad.'

'Rankin I'm not letting you wander off into the woods in the dark. The pig'll turn up in the morning. Think he'd miss his breakfast.'

Rankin called again. All was silent but for the buzz of crickets. Ophelia laid a hand on his shoulder and pulled him back toward the porch.

'That was Reives out there tonight,' he said.

'I don't doubt it. Ya'll get back to bed now. We'll see about the pig in the morning.'

But there was no sign of Traveller at sun up. Rankin had already dressed and was going out the door when I awoke. I got up and went into the kitchen. Ophelia was there making coffee. Together we sat and waited for almost an hour until Rankin returned, his shoes soaked from the dew.

'I walked all the way up to town. Not a sign of him.'

Ophelia poured him a glass of orange juice, and he slumped down in a chair.

'There's blood out in the grass. Told you he was hurt.'

Ophelia sighed.

'Have some breakfast now and then we'll all go out looking.'

Later that morning when we were about to set off across the pasture I decided to check around the front of the house. That's where I found Traveller. He was lying on his side under the front porch, a large patch of blood soaking into the dirt beneath his snout.

Ophelia phoned the local vet, Dr Landry. Rankin crouched under the porch with Traveller all the rest of that morning.

Soon after lunch Landry's red Dodge truck rattled up in front of the house. He called from the driver's window.

'Got a sick hog?'

'That's right,' said Ophelia.

Landry climbed out the pick-up and removed his suit jacket, hanging it carefully on a shotgun rack in his back windshield. He was a small stocky man, with close-cropped blond hair and round wire-rimmed glasses. No matter how dirty the task at hand Dr Landry always made a point of being well turned out: fine linen suits, bow ties and suspenders, a fresh handkerchief in his top pocket. He grabbed his instrument case from inside a steel storage bin in the back of the truck, and then slipped a stained leather apron over his white cotton shirt.

'Let's see if we can't coax him out here in the open,' he said, peering under the porch.

Rankin and I managed to get Traveller on his feet. Long strings of reddish-black mucus trailed from his mouth. He stumbled out into the grass and collapsed. Landry gently lifted the bloody upper lip.

'Looks to me like your pig's taken a swift kick to the jaw. You got a temperamental horse around here?'

'No sir,' said Rankin.

Landry gave him a quizzical look. Ophelia put in:

'More like a temperamental neighbor.'

'You sure about that?'

'Think so.'

Landry examined the mouth again.

'Suppose it's possible – with a strong boot.'

'Will he be okay?' Rankin asked.

'Lost a fair amount of blood. The inside of the lip is torn clean away. The jaw might be fractured. Lets have a better look.'

He sedated Traveller and then cleaned the wound with hydrogen peroxide before stitching it up.

'Can't really tell about the jaw without X-rays but it seems okay. You got a tap somewhere?'

Landry washed his hands under the faucet at the side of the house. Then gathering up his instruments he walked back to the truck and slipped on his suit jacket.

'You're going to have to watch for infection. Give him dry feed well-soaked in milk – no swill – and plenty of fresh water. I'll be back in a day or so to check on him.'

Landry climbed into the pick-up and started the engine. He hesitated a moment and then leaned out the window.

'Maybe you ought to call the sheriff. No reason for this sort of foolishness.'

He gave us a brisk salute and the Dodge pulled away.

Ophelia went straight back into the house and pulled out the phone book. Finding the listing for the Folsom Sheriff Department, she lifted the receiver.

'Your daddy'd probably not approve. But that man just can't go getting away with this.'

Later that afternoon a white squad car drew up at the side of the house. A short, dumpy looking man about age sixty climbed up onto the porch and knocked at the door. He had thick grey hair and a mustache. Other than a blue shirt with a cloth badge sewn on one shoulder, little else marked him as a law officer: no gun belt, no handcuffs, no night stick. He wore faded khaki trousers and a pair of old work boots. Even his straw hat was not regulation, and he clutched it in his hands as Ophelia led him into the front room. Taking a seat on the couch, he pulled out a small black notebook. I noticed the name Pechon stitched above his shirt pocket.

Ophelia provided most of the details, which he scribbled into the notebook in a neat shorthand.

'So who actually owns the pig?' He then asked.

'I do,' said Rankin.

Sheriff Pechon glanced up at my brother. He then flipped shut the notebook and stuck it in his back pocket.

'Let's have a look at him.'

Traveller had retreated back under the steps. Sheriff Pechon squatted down under the floorboards. The bleeding had stopped except for a small trickle leaking from one nostril. But Traveller's snout was now grossly swollen, an angry purple in colour.

'He's sure taken a nasty shot. You got any horses around here.'

'No sir,' said Rankin.

'Cows?'

'No sir, only chickens.'

Sheriff Pechon narrowed his eyes.

'Got to ask you these questions son.'

'Why? You know who did it. Just go arrest him.'

'It's not that simple.'

The sheriff grabbed the edge of the porch and pulled himself back up with a groan. Ophelia offered him a glass of iced tea.

'No thank you. Think I'll go on over and have a talk with Gilbert. Let me tell you this ain't the first time. I'll call back on my way out.'

Sheriff Pechon left his car and limped up the drive toward Reives' house. Rankin and I sat out on the front steps waiting. Nearly half an hour went by before he returned. He pulled up a rocking chair on the porch and fanned himself with his hat.

'Reives says he was in his bed by ten o'clock last night. Told me the last watermelon he stole was about forty years ago.'

'Well he's lying,' said Rankin. 'I heard his voice out in the yard.'

'So you say.'

'Did you talk to Alice, his daughter?' Ophelia asked.

'Didn't see her.'

'She might tell you the truth.'

Sheriff Pechon slowly wiped his brow with a handkerchief.

'Listen. I don't think much good'll come of pursuing this. Gilbert's mad as hell, and to be honest I'm less worried now about what he's done than what he might do.'

Rankin bristled:

'But you know it was him.'

'Son, I only know what you told me, and I can't charge him just on the basis of that.'

'That's bullshit!'

Ophelia leapt up.

'You get in the house right this minute boy!'

Rankin slammed the door behind him.

'I'm so sorry. I've never seen him like this before.'

Pechon waved both hands.

'Don't worry. I hear much worse than that just about every Saturday night.'

Ophelia sat down again and spoke quietly.

'I understand what you're saying about Mr Reives. We just don't want that man coming around here no more.'

'Well I warned him. So all you do is call me if he much as looks over your fence.'

Sheriff Pechon then stood up and hobbled off the porch. Before getting back in the squad car he took one last look under the steps at Traveller.

'I do feel for the boy. That's a fine animal.'

We never did find out exactly what happened that night out in the yard. But the way I imagine it is this: Reives must have staggered over from his porch, well fortified with cheap bourbon. Maybe he'd just intended to steal the watermelon, or maybe he had something else in mind. In any case he must of hefted it over the edge of the fence and stood there swaying in the moonlight, unaware that Traveller was watching, the shape of that watermelon triggering a particular memory in that active brain. Reives probably never heard him coming, charging silently over the thick grass. One second he was standing, the next flat on his back, with the watermelon lying broken in the dirt beside him.

Traveller probably thought it was a gift, or some incredible piece of good fortune. Maybe he'd already sunk his teeth into the sweet rind, just as the boot struck.

Chapter 12

I had a dream once as a child in which our mother had never died in that accident at Edgard. Rankin and I are going to visit her for the first time. For some odd reason the hospital is out on an island in the middle of a swamp. To get there my father has had to borrow Mr Wingfield's bass boat. We glide down a flooded bayou through thick cypress. Snakes and turtles slide into the brown water as we pass. Eventually the bayou opens out into a broad marsh. Ducks and geese fly overhead like in one of my grandfather's watercolors.

The island rises above the sedge grass and cat-tails ahead. A complex of low pine buildings – like barracks – stands on the high ground. Drawing near we see a nun in a black habit waiting for us on a wooden pier. My father draws up and ties the boat. The nun turns silently and leads us towards one of the buildings. The hospital grounds are drab and depressing – bright green lawns transected with paths of hot concrete.

Reaching the entrance the nun turns to us and raises a

finger to her lips. Then she opens the door and leads us into a large room full of wheezing iron lungs. It looks like a photo of a children's polio ward I had once seen in *Life* magazine. My excitement and curiosity turn instantly to dread. Yet Rankin has a smile on his face and looks around expectantly. He carries a bunch of flowers.

The nun beckons us to a corner which has been partitioned off from the rest of the room. Behind the curtain is another of the huge lungs. From where we stand only her long brown hair is visible falling over the pillow. The nun reaches above the cylinder to adjust a mirror and our mother's face appears, framed in the glass much as it is in Rankin's bedside portrait at home.

But it's a different face – one altered with age and sickness. The skin sags off her cheeks in sallow folds. Her eyes are hollow and ringed in dark circles. Worst of all though is her expression – one of languid bitterness.

'Who are these people?' She asks the nun in a tired whisper.

'These are your children, Mrs Calhoun.'

'Children? I don't remember having children. Is this some kind of joke.'

Rankin pushes forward.

'But you have to remember me?'

She squints into the mirror.

'Why I've never laid eyes on you.'

'But you have to.'

Our dream mother then closes her eyes and sighs:

'Sister. Is a little peace and quiet too much to ask?'

That's all I can remember apart from waking up with an odd surge of tenderness towards my brother asleep in the next bed, something much deeper and stronger than the day-to-day hatred he usually inspired in me.

*

An infection developed in Traveller's jaw which began to gradually poison his system. The pig stopped eating the milky feed which Rankin brought, and over the next few days grew too weak to even stand. Although we tried to keep a bed of fresh hay under the porch, the dirt soon formed into a foul-smelling mire. Rankin tramped through it almost hourly in his filthy hunting boots, each time raising a cloud of flies as he brought water which the pig drank by the bucket-full.

Dr Landry visited the farm again in a few days. That morning he wore a light blue Haspel suit tucked into a pair of Hunter Wellington boots. He crouched under the porch to examine Traveller's mouth.

'Think maybe he's needing something a little stronger.'

Landry went back to his truck and returned with two glass vials and a syringe. Then drawing up a dose of antibiotics, he said to Rankin:

'Watch me now. You'll have to do it the next time.'

He popped the needle into Traveller's haunch.

'Easy as that. Think you can give him two of those a day.'

Rankin nodded.

'Good. Now it's important he gets back on the feed. Try giving him just milk for a while. I'll be back in a day or two.'

Landry offered no estimate of Traveller's chances. Rankin never asked. For the past two days he'd hardly spoken a word to anyone. It was an angry, stubborn silence. Ophelia only just managed to keep her patience.

'No sense acting this way,' she finally said, one evening at dinner. 'We're just as upset.'

But Rankin only stared at his plate a moment and then asked to be excused.

Later that same day after Dr Landry's visit, Tyler showed up at the house. He peered under the porch at Traveller and pinched his nose.

'What a stink!'

I expected Rankin to punch him. Instead he pulled Tyler

aside and whispered into his ear. The two of them then headed off toward the barn. When I made to follow, Rankin turned and pointed a warning finger at me.

'No snitches allowed this time.'

So I could honestly say I knew nothing of the scheme he and Tyler hatched that afternoon up in the loft.

That evening after dinner Rankin complained it was too hot inside and asked permission to sleep out on the back porch. Ophelia suggested we both make beds out there – to Rankin's clear annoyance. Wishing us good night she shut the back door and turned out the light. Outside it was humid and overcast – the moon glowing through a thick bank of clouds. Rankin turned on his side and fell instantly asleep.

Later that night I awoke with a start to find Rankin sitting up, fully dressed, tying his shoes.

'What are you doing?'

He leaned close to my ear.

'You just lie there quiet, Milo – or else. I'm just going out to check on Traveller.'

The screen door creaked as he slipped out into the night. I knew that he was lying. For nearly half an hour I lay awake on the mattress, waiting for him to return. Then I must have dozed off.

A muffled boom pulled me out of a shallow sleep. I sat upright not quite certain what had caused the sound. A few minutes later I heard someone running across the grass. Tyler threw open the screen door. He was out of breath, hardly able to speak.

'Better wake up Ophelia.'

But Ophelia was already awake. She ran out on to the porch.

'What you doing here Tyler? Where's Rankin?'

'I think Reives got him.'

'What you mean got him? Tell me what you been up to.'

'It was Rankin's idea. We snuck over there.'

'You did what?'

'Snuck over to let loose that white racoon – cause of Traveller.'

Tyler began to sob.

'Reives shot me. Look!'

He pulled up the back of his shirt.

'Am I bleeding?'

'No you not bleeding,' snapped Ophelia. 'Now where's Rankin?'

'Last I saw he was still trying to get the racoon out. I think Reives caught him.'

'Ya'll wait here,' said Ophelia, and she hurried back into house.

A few seconds later she returned wearing a pair of unlaced work boots, though still in her dressing gown.

'Come on.'

All the lights were burning at the Reives' house. Gilbert was sitting out on the porch waiting for us. Ophelia walked straight through the gate and up to the house.

'Where's Rankin?'

Reives stood up slowly and smiled, a shotgun cradled over his arm.

'I'm asking you where's Rankin?'

'Never you mind,' he said. 'It's me who's getting the sheriff this time.'

'You bring him out here now. The sheriff can come see him down at our place.'

'No. I think we'll just do it my way this time.'

'Well then I'm coming in to get him myself.'

Ophelia started toward the porch. Reives levelled his shotgun.

'Take one step on them boards, nigger.'

Just then Alice appeared in the doorway.

'Put that down,' she cried. 'For God's sake – haven't you done enough already?'

Reives swung around in sudden fury and drew back

his hand. But just at that moment Rankin dashed out from around the side of house. Ophelia shouted to him to wait but Rankin never hesitated, bolting through the gate and down the road. She turned back to Reives.

'What did you do to that child?'

'Only defending my property.'

Ophelia stood there a moment, frozen in anger.

'Tell you what,' she then said. 'Touch one of these children again and you *will* have to use that shotgun on me.'

'Fine by me,' replied Reives. 'What's one less nigger maid in this world.'

But Ophelia had already turned away and was hustling Tyler and me back up the path. Once we'd reached the cattle guard I looked back through the trees to the lighted porch and dreaded to think what might happen to Alice that night. Ophelia followed my gaze with much the same thought.

Back home we found Rankin curled up on top of his bed. Ophelia sat next to him and smoothed back his hair. A plug of crusted blood choked one of his nostrils, and a small purple bruise was forming under his right eye.

Ophelia sighed:

'What makes you want to go heaping trouble upon sadness.'

Something then seemed to give way in my brother and he began to cry in breathless sobs. Ophelia hugged him like a small child.

'You too young for all this heartache.'

Tyler stood next to me in the doorway, his ears scarlet with embarrassment. I was the only one to notice when he slipped out the front door into the early morning. I lay down on the couch and fell asleep. Just how long she sat with him I can't say. It was past dawn when I heard Ophelia in the kitchen filling the kettle.

Just after nine that next morning Sheriff Pechon arrived. Ophelia met him out by the car and they spoke for a few moments before coming into the house. She then went to wake up Rankin. Pechon sat down on the couch and began to thumb through a copy of *Boy's Life*. Soon he was engrossed in an article on flat water canoeing. He seemed almost reluctant to lay aside the magazine when my brother came into the room. Rankin sat quietly on the edge of my father's arm chair.

'So I hear you paid a late night visit up the road there.'
'Yes sir.'
'Come over here.'

Rankin stood up and walked to the side of the couch. Sheriff Pechon slipped on his spectacles. He reached under Rankin's chin and turned his cheek.

'Reives do this to you?'

Rankin nodded.

'Then maybe you better tell me exactly what happened.'

Rankin went back to the chair and spoke hardly above a whisper. He told the sheriff how he and Tyler had met out by the barn that night and then snuck through the woods, up to the back of Reives' house. Rankin had wanted only to open the door to the racoon cage so the animal could escape – nothing more. But pulling the wool blanket off the top they found the hatch padlocked. Tyler had wanted to go home at that point. But Rankin decided to look for a pair of wire cutters in Reives' shed.

Pushing open the door he upset a steel feed bucket from a high shelf – or maybe Reives had put it over the door as a poor man's burglar alarm. It banged down loudly onto the wood floor. Tyler turned to run. But Rankin hesitated and watched the house for a minute or so. No lights came on. So he went back into the shed with his flashlight and found a pair of metal shears hanging on a nail. He cut a large hole in the chicken wire and pulled back the flap. But the racoon would not come near the opening. It just kept pacing back and forth across the rear of the cage.

So Tyler wandered out into the yard to find a stick to prod the animal out. This was when Reives appeared from around the side of the house – the shotgun in his hands. Tyler first shouted to Rankin and then tore off across the yard. He was almost to the woods before Reives fired.

Rankin stood by the cage, too frightened to move. Reives pushed the shotgun barrel against his chest and bent the flap of chicken wire back in place.

'Maybe I should just shoot you now,' he said. 'I'd be in my rights.'

Instead he pulled my brother into that tool shed and beat him almost senseless, first with a broken cane fishing pole and then with his hands. Alice must have heard the cries. She pounded on the door and pleaded for him to stop. Eventually Reives tired himself out. He yanked Rankin into the house and pushed him into a closet, and jammed a chair under the door knob. It was only later when Ophelia arrived that Alice got her chance to let him out.

Rankin did not stop running until he'd reached the house. There, leaning over the edge of the front porch, he'd emptied his stomach into the grass.

Sheriff Pechon opened his notebook and wrote down a few details. Then he put it back in his pocket and stared hard at Rankin.

'So what are we gonna do, son?' He asked. 'You were trespassing. Vandalizing that man's property.'

Rankin glanced over at Ophelia. She turned away and stared out the window.

'Reives might have shot you in the dark, and maybe even justified it. We'd only have his word. But as things turned out he beat you around some. Now I'm not saying anybody deserves that, but you were damn lucky.

Sheriff Pechon then pulled a half-smoked cigar from his top pocket and stood up.

'Now I'm gonna go have a talk with the man. Probably I'll be able to convince him that it ain't worth pressing charges against you and your buddy Fendleson – considering I could charge him for assaulting a minor. You follow me?'

Rankin nodded.

'So we'll just forget about it this time. But listen here: I don't want you to ever be the cause of me coming out here again. Keep away from Gilbert Reives. Now I best go clear up this mess.'

Later that afternoon Ophelia called my father. Having the sheriff out to the house was regarded as serious enough to warrant his driving up after work. Not even Ophelia had wanted that. She served our dinner early and laid a plate aside. Rankin did not touch his food. I remember stealing glances across the table at him, less with sympathy than a sort of tremulous awe.

Near seven we heard the Oldsmobile pull up outside. My father slammed the car door, then coming up the steps he paused. Ophelia flinched – ever so slightly. The door swung open.

'Can somebody tell me what this smell is out here.'

George leaned through the doorway.

'Ophelia?'

'Right here Mr Calhoun,' she answered wearily. 'That'd be the pig under the porch. I told you on the phone he was sick.'

'But not under the floorboards for God's sake. Did you tell Rankin he could keep that animal under here.'

'Not much chance of us moving him.'

'Tell you what. Joe will – in the morning with the tractor. I'm calling the vet out. That animal's caused enough problems around here. Now can I get some dinner?'

Ophelia shook her head and disappeared into the kitchen. My father turned to Rankin.

'You and I will talk later. Go on to your room.'

George then had his meal in the kitchen. Ophelia sat at

the table and told him the full story. From where I sat in the den I could only hear the tone of their voices. My father's angry and incredulous. Ophelia's quiet but firm.

Only later, after an hour in the den with his newspaper, did my father finally call for Rankin. My brother's eyes were red and swollen, his face pale. George took off his glasses and laid them on the table next to his armchair.

'You know I got in some trouble once,' he began. 'I was only a couple years older than you. Went joy-riding in an old colored man's truck with some friends. It wasn't much of a truck – but the sheriff chased us down. Called all our parents.

'That night my father came home and made me cut a big green switch off a crepe myrtle tree. He took me out to the barn and whipped the daylights out of me. Told me to stay out there, that that's where I belonged, with the rest of the animals. Dinner time passed and nobody came for me. Then it started getting late. Finally around midnight I looked out and saw all the lights off in the house. I walked up to the back door and found it locked. Went around the front and found that one locked too. So you know what – I spent the night out in that barn, cold and miserable. Now being locked out your own house – that was much worse than any whipping. But I got the message. My father was not going to tolerate that kind of behavior.'

George got up and poured himself a glass of scotch.

'Ophelia told me what happened. You know what I think? I think Reives was perfectly justified in what he did. Sneaking up to his house like that, damaging his property'.

Rankin stared down at his shoes and muttered:

'So you want me to go sleep out in the barn?'

'What did you say?'

Rankin looked up and spoke louder:

'Do you want me to sleep in the barn?'

'Maybe so. Maybe it'd do you some good.'

'I don't mind. I'll sleep under the porch – the smell don't bother me.'

'Fine then smartass – just get the hell on out of here.'

Rankin stood up and walked slowly across the room.

'You don't even have to lock the door.'

That was enough for my father. He slammed down his whiskey and sprung out of the chair.

'Get over here.'

Rankin made no effort to escape. George unbuckled his thin leather belt and yanked Rankin to the centre of the room. What he said then was as unexpected as it was cruel.

'God help me – but you are just your mother through and through. Spoiled, deceitful, not a care for anyone else in this world, least of all her own family – that was your mother.'

'No,' Rankin sobbed. 'You're a liar.'

'Oh, let me tell you son. Cry all night. It won't change a damn thing. Now you pull down those trousers.'

George removed his belt and doubled it over. Rankin slid his jeans down over his knees. A look of sudden perplexity then came over my father's face, and he slowly lowered his hand. The welts formed a criss-cross pattern up the back of Rankin's thighs and across his buttocks – a tic-tac-toe of red and purple bruises. George reached out and lifted his tee-shirt. There were more marks across Rankin's lower back. A few moments passed and he sighed:

'Go on to bed now.'

Rankin pulled up his jeans without a word and went back to his room. My father sat down heavily in his chair and had a sip of scotch, the belt still in his hand. For perhaps the first time in my life I thought I saw a hint of self-doubt, a shadow of confusion cross my father's face. I found it oddly unsettling – almost more so than the marks on Rankin's skin.

He just then seemed to notice that I was still in the room. His eyes dropped.

'You go on too son. Bedtime.'

Chapter 13

Almost seven years would pass before I understood the bitterness that lay behind my father's words that night. Enlightenment came from an unlikely source. I was sixteen years old and a Junior at De La Salle High, an all-boys school run by the Christian Brothers on St Charles Avenue. That spring a guidance counselor named Brother Ben Emile encouraged me to get involved in a program known as Youth Achievement America.

YAA involved local business people who helped students form mini-companies that would produce some service or manufactured product. Dogwashing, scented candles, bits of turned wood sold as salad spoons were the usual things, all foisted mainly on family friends and relatives. The program aimed to provide practical experience for the 'business leaders of the 1980s and 90s' – a slightly sinister thought in retrospect. But Brother Ben insisted it would look wonderful on my college applications. Other schools in the local area were also involved, including Sacred Heart, Ursuline and a few other private girls' academies. This was the prime attraction of YAA to the young men of De La Salle.

A hundred or so students filled the cafeteria at Sacred Heart that first afternoon. Looking over the various cliques that milled about the room I spotted a familiar face. Laurel Anderson no longer resembled her younger sister Britain. Gone were the pageboy haircuts and Ep's matching outfits. Laurel had grown into a tall leggy teenager with long auburn hair and a thin attractive face. I'd heard somewhere that she suffered from an 'eating disorder' but I thought she was beautiful, if untouchable. Ep's hatred for me had not eased over the years and our family had little to do with the Andersons, especially since they'd moved Uptown to State Street.

Each YAA member was given an index card printed with a letter of the alphabet so that we could be divided randomly into 10 companies. Our adult 'consultants' held up placards and I made my way to 'D Company' and a large heavy-set man in a pinstripe suit. He wore a crewcut and had a stick-on lapel label that read 'Hello, My Name is Mr Felker.'

Among the other 'student directors' in the company was Laurel. At first I thought she had not recognized me. But as the meeting broke up and we all headed through the cafeteria doors she turned and spoke.

'David Calhoun.'

An almost hostile look passed over her face; her brown eyes darted nervously across mine. Not even the hint of a smile appeared on her lips.

'Hi Laurel,' I said.

But she had already set off across the campus with two of her girlfriends.

At the next meeting Mr Felker encouraged us to brainstorm ideas for a possible product. Although a seasoned

marketing executive at Walgreens Drugs, he looked distinct-
ly uncomfortable before this small group of teenagers. As he
spoke patches of sweat formed under his arms and down the
center of his back.

Eventually we settled on a gift item: a bar of cheap scented
soap tied with brown twine to a scallop shell (obtained free
from a local seafood outlet). Mr Felker was beside himself
with delight. Here, he said, was the very essence of good
marketing – 'to enhance the perceived value of a product by
a smart concept and clever packaging'.

'Look at the pet rock phenomenon,' he enthused.

'A round pebble and a few pennies' worth of paint and
these things were selling for a dollar fifty each!'

Our next task was to come up with a name for our
product.

'Don't settle for just some bland description,' advised Mr
Felker.

'Choose a dynamic name, one that suggests excitement
and pleasure to the buyer. Think of Chanel perfumes, Dodge
Charger, Timberland Cologne. Think of Brute, My Sin.
You're not just selling a bar of soap tied to an old shell –
you're selling an image.'

Mr Felker then encouraged us to brainstorm 'key words'
to do with our product. He picked up a piece of chalk and
drew a column on the blackboard.

'Shout out anything – no matter how silly. I'll write them
down and we'll sort through the list afterwards.'

A few of the more keen YAAers began calling out words.

'Suds, lather, clean, fresh, zest, vitality . . .'

I had begun to regret having ever listened to Brother
Ben. Looking across the room I saw Laurel staring quietly
out the window. Just then a bubbly senior from the Ursuline
Convent School began to sing out words faster than Mr
Felker could write.

'Sea, sand, shell, pearl, parcel, string, twine, tie, bind,
bound . . .'

She hesitated an instant, her mouth still moving soundlessly. Mr Felker grinned and beckoned gently with his fingers.

'Bondage!'

The room went silent. Mr Felker's hand froze against the blackboard and his cheeks grew crimson. A moment passed. Both Laurel and I then burst out laughing. No one else dared.

Next meeting I asked Laurel out to a movie at the Prytania Theater. Soon we were seeing each other every weekend. I would pick her up at a girlfriend's in my father's old Le Sabre and we'd go to the Camelia Grill or Bud's Broiler or out to Lakeside Cinema.

Both of us had a literary bent and we talked mostly about books and movies. *The Bell Jar* was her favorite novel, which struck me then as pretty disturbing. I also discovered that Laurel had an all-abiding hatred for both her mother and her sister Megan who was now playing the Southern Belle at Princeton University. Neither ever found out about us though – even after we broke up before my Freshman year in college.

One Friday night not long after our first date we went to see a movie in Metairie and afterwards parked along the Lake Pontchartrain Levee. It was a warm evening and we sat on the hood of the car looking out across the dark water. Somehow the conversation got around to my father. Laurel commented that to her George had always seemed such a sad, disappointed man. I thought this was an odd thing to say. Sure my father had faced some bad times, I agreed, particularly the accident. But there was nothing much for him to be disappointed about. He thrived on hard work and had always been successful in his business.

'But the circumstances were so awful,' Laurel persisted. 'All that gossip.'

An odd crawling sensation spread across the skin of my back.

'What gossip?'

Laurel turned away. I could see the flush in her cheeks.

'It's probably all lies,' she muttered. 'Just one of my mother's favorite cocktail stories.'

'What are you talking about?' I pressed.

This was when I first heard the saga that had been embellished for years among the Uptown set. Ep had told it so often to dinner guests that Laurel knew her mother's version almost word for word.

The fact is Margot Aubry never truly loved my father – or so it goes. Long before she met George, back still at McGehee's, my mother fell in with a boy named Hollis Reed. This was the same Hollis mentioned in that postcard Gerry Whitney wrote my mother from Rome.

The Reeds were a prominent family – Hollis' father owned a sugar cane plantation in Terrebonne Parish. His mother was a Whitney (he and Gerry were cousins). But Hollis himself was a bit of a tearaway by reputation – disrespectful, a party boy and a compulsive liar. All through senior high and most of college he and Margot maintained a turbulent liaison. Hollis supposedly once slapped her in public at a debutante ball in the functions room of the Chase Library.

I found a photograph of him in one of Big Mum's scrapbooks. It was in a newspaper clipping from the society page of the *States Item*. A group of couples is standing by a fountain. Margot's arm is intertwined with that of a tall thin young man in a white evening suit. His hair and eyes are dark, and his face smooth and handsome.

Big Mum apparently could not bear the sight of Hollis,

who she predicted would end up either a crooked politician or in prison. Hollis was forbidden from the house and on the telephone. The incident at the Chase Ball was the final straw.

Soon after, my mother began dating George – to Big Mum's immense relief. Margot agreed to marry my father but it was obvious that she had not gotten over her obsession with Hollis.

When Rankin was born my mother seemed to settle for a while. But then just after I came along she learned that Hollis had become engaged to marry a girl from Natchez, Mississippi. She had already been taking medication to counter post-natal depression. The news supposedly drove her completely mad.

She wrote Hollis a long letter telling him how it had been a terrible mistake marrying George. Hollis had only to say the word and she would leave the three of us. But he wrote back and told her not to be so ridiculous and pathetic, that he no longer had the slightest feeling for her, that even when they had dated it was never more than a childish affair.

My mother was utterly distraught the day of the accident. To top it all Ruby had called in sick that morning. She managed to leave Rankin with Mrs Favret next door but decided to take me along to Gerry's. All that afternoon the two of them drank sloe gin and argued over my mother's dilemma. Margot finally decided that she had to see Hollis face to face.

Gerry claims she tried to stop my mother from taking me out to the Buick. But gossip has it that she was too drunk to care. I've met the woman only once – a tall willowy figure with a deep tan and striking blue eyes. Ophelia had dropped Rankin and me at a birthday party at Orleans Country Club. She was coming out of the dining room and recognized Rankin.

'Well hello there,' she drawled and then laid a hand lightly on my shoulder.

'This can't be David? You don't know me but I'm your

wicked Aunt Gerry. Last time I saw you it was in a little diaper.'

She then floated past us out the door and climbed into her husband's Mercedes. No doubt she's still withering away somewhere in the Garden District.

In any case, my mother left the Whitneys' late that afternoon and drove across the Huey P. Long Bridge to look for the Reed Mansion out along River Road. Even if she had managed to find the house it's said that Hollis was away that weekend water skiing.

Ep Anderson – at this point in the story – always left it up to her guests to decide whether it really had been an accident after all. Margot Aubry wandering lost and miserable over those backroads, me in the back seat screaming blue murder – maybe she just closed her eyes and let go of the steering wheel.

Just how much of this is true I cannot say. I have never confronted my father with these details and never will. Nor have I asked him about the letters Rankin thought he saw George tearing up after my mother's funeral. But I often think back to that night after Sheriff Pechon's visit to the farm, and those words my father used to batter Rankin as soundly as he could have with any belt.

That next morning George returned to New Orleans before anyone was awake. All day we waited for Dr Landry to come put Traveller down. But he never showed up; nor did he come the next day or the next.

Traveller grew no better over that period – and yet grew no worse. Then one morning a few days later he took a little milk and that afternoon ate some soft feed. The next day he managed to struggle up from his fetid sick patch and stumble across the yard to the water trough for a long drink.

Saturday morning Dr Landry's truck finally rattled into the yard. It was stifling hot and the vet had left his jacket at home. But he still wore a bow tie and a pair of natty baby blue and white striped suspenders.

'Looks as though he's past the worst of it,' said Landry, strolling up to Traveller's pen. 'Takes a while sometimes for the antibiotics to catch hold.'

Rankin stood in front of the gate with a scowl. Landry smiled quizically.

'Something wrong with you boy?'

'Didn't my father call you?'

'Nobody called me. I told ya'll last week I'd be back to take the stitches out.'

Landry then stepped past my brother through the gate and laid his bag down. He snipped the threads out from beneath Traveller's lip, and then went over to a corner of the pen and stirred some manure with the toe of his boot.

'Not the sweetest smell but at least it's healthy.'

We hadn't seen Tyler all that week. This was odd considering that scarcely a day had passed that summer without him eating at least one meal at our house. Ophelia had grounded Rankin for what in effect was the rest of the summer. So one day about a week before we were due to return to New Orleans, I paid a visit on my own to the Fendlesons.

Tyler met me at the back door. Miss Sis called out from inside the kitchen:

'Who's that, son?'

'Just David.'

'Well tell him he can only stay a half hour.'

Tyler nodded, rolling his eyes, and pushed me back outside. Things had not gone well for him that week. It turned out that Sheriff Pechon had also paid the Fendlesons a visit just after he left our farm. Miss Sis had not taken the news well.

'Pechon had to bring her a chair,' said Tyler. 'Thought she felt faint. You'd think I'd held-up Marslan's or something.

Then my daddy comes home and belts me so hard I had to sleep on my stomach. I'm not allowed to leave the farm again until school starts up.'

Charlie Brown had begun to whine and bark at us.

'Tell you what, much more of this and I'll end up one of them kids that murders his family in the dead of night – dog and all.'

Tyler looked at his watch.

'Oh yea. Almost forgot the best.'

He then led me out to the snake shed and pushed open the door. Inside the floor was littered with shattered glass and pine straw. The far shelf was cleared of cages. A puddle of murky water lay in the center of the concrete floor.

'My father found it like this. Then killed my king snake. Said he thought it was poisonous. Dummkopf.'

'What about the pictures?'

'Gone.'

Tyler reached down to pick up a dead frog and threw it out the doorway.

'Best that I can figure is Steve Finch blabbed to Bone – unless ya'll did. He's the only other one I showed 'em to. This morning my daddy tells me to make sure I catch every last snake – before momma finds out. Had to let them all loose down by the swamp.'

Tyler then spotted a small aquarium on the floor across the room. A long crack stretched across one side, but it was otherwise sound. He stepped over the broken glass and lifted it onto a shelf.

'Hey, maybe I can use this one again.'

Chapter 14

Judge Edmund J. Taylor ends his loving description of the 'modern hog farm' with a chapter entitled simply 'The Harvest'. As in other chapters the lyrical intertwines the practical – in this case a detailed assessment of high-tensile bone saws, steel skewers and Swiss-made meat cleavers.

Reaching the end of the chapter and the close of this masterpiece of his declining years, the Judge felt moved to comment on 'a curious dichotomy' present throughout the text. That is his love of the animal character ('Old Abe's cheery grunt on a frosty Delta morning') in seeming opposition to his fondness for hickory-cured bacon. He writes:

'A farm animal has no being outwith the farm. Its lineage, breed, its very existence is derived completely from its utility. To ignore this, to allow any sentiment beyond common affection is to devalue that animal, to render it trivial, obsolete. Nothing strikes me as more degrading than talking horses on moving picture screens, or painted pigs dancing for their fodder in the circus ring. A boar sports his nobility in the open field, but yields his raison d' être in the smokehouse.'

No doubt the judge would have felt our family pig ill-used, for Traveller never made it to the butcher's. That summer he recovered from Gilbert's kick with only a slightly crooked snout, and over the next few years grew to an immense size. Each May he'd greet our arrival for the summer with a leaden frolic, and for the next three months would savor Ophelia's rich leftovers, lounging in the dusty shade of the house, rousing himself only occasionally to stir up the chickens.

Those months we weren't at the farm, Traveller had the run of the place. Joe Dreux came each day with feed for him and my father's fifteen or so head of cattle (none of these escaped the slaughter house). In that sense he proved better than a watch dog. Though more curious than aggressive, he was 800lbs of curious. Even my father grew accustomed to having Traveller around the place, and over time the pig took to following George on his weekly circuit of the fields like an old trusted dog.

Traveller lived on content at Buck Falaya until one late October day in 1971. I was a sophomore then at De La Salle and Rankin had started his freshman year at Vanderbilt in Nashville. It was a Sunday morning and my father had a call from Joe Dreaux to tell us our pig was dead. It was as plain as that. Joe was never very good on the telephone and refused to hazard a guess as to how or why. My father asked him to meet us at the farm that afternoon.

Ophelia came over after Mass to bring a roast she'd cooked for our Sunday dinner. She was married then, nearly two years. Her husband Robert was a plumber, and their first daughter Ellen was just a baby. They lived on Kingston Street just off Claiborne, though Ophelia still drove out to cook for us three afternoons a week, stacking the fridge with plastic tubs of gumbo and red beans and rice that we had not a hope of ever getting through.

That morning Ophelia had planned only to drop off the roast, and had left Robert in the car with the baby. Hearing the news, though, she sat a moment in the kitchen with us and drank a cup of coffee.

'Have you called Rankin yet?'

'No,' said George. 'Didn't see any point in ruining the whole Sunday for him.'

'Guess not.'

No one spoke for a few moments and the kitchen was silent but for the ticking of the oven timer.

'Really, I best get home now,' Ophelia said finally, and dabbed at a tear that was spoiling her make up. She gathered up her purse and hat, and waved goodbye at the door.

Joe's truck was parked in front of the house when we drove into the farm. A mechanical digger sat on a trailer hitched at the back. The air was clear and cold, the first real touch of Fall. Joe climbed out the cab of the pick-up and met us at the front steps.

'Around back,' he said.

Traveller sat in the grass about ten yards from the kitchen door, his chin resting across his forehocks as though napping. I knelt down and laid my hand on his back. It was cold as stone.

'Think it could have been a heart attack?' My father asked.

Joe shook his head and pointed to a small red spot just below Traveller's left ear. It was a tiny hole, only just a trickle of blood. Joe reckoned a 22 calibre bullet, a clean shot at close range. I found it odd to imagine how a wound that small could bring down such a huge figure.

My father called the Folsom Police Department. Sheriff Pechon had since retired, and the deputy who came out was a much younger man, clean shaven, with the regulation uniform, hat and gun belt. He never removed his sunglasses during the entire visit.

It seemed fairly obvious that Gilbert Reives was the culprit. Over the years his malice toward our family had only grown worse. Not long after the summer of 1965, Alice left Buck Falaya and moved to Vicksburg to live with her aunt. She and Ophelia still exchanged Christmas cards. Reives blamed us for this and most everything else. His drinking grew heavier and the shack began to fall down around him. Two years later he would finally die from liver failure; it was amazing he'd lasted that long. But in 1971 he was still roaming the town, picking up his welfare check and the daily pint of Wild Turkey.

The deputy took a cursory look around the yard and then told us we'd never be able to prove that Reives had fired the shot.

'Nearly every farm in the area's got a 22 rifle,' he said. 'And besides, ya'll got kinda a reputation around here.'

So the deputy left Buck Falaya without even knocking on Gilbert's door.

Later that afternoon we picked out a spot near the edge of the pasture, and Joe dug a deep trench with the John Deere. We looped a rope around Traveller's forehocks, and Joe dragged him behind the tractor across the yard. It took all three of us to roll the pig into the grave. The ground shuddered when Traveller hit the moist clay at the bottom.

Joe replaced the dirt with the mechanical digger while my father and I helped with shovels. Soon rain would level the dirt and grass would grow over the spot, leaving only a slight depression in the ground.

That evening driving back across Lake Pontchartrain my father and I said little. Near the south shore George turned off the radio.

'Maybe I'll just call your brother in the morning.'

But Rankin would have guessed something was wrong.

My father had taken to phoning him every Sunday night since he went away to college. He'd ask Rankin about this or that exam, or if he was keeping his hair cut. George had also begun to complain to me about how quiet the house was. He said I read too many books.

Later that evening I searched through the desk in the den and found a blank post-card of the Steamboat Natchez. I wrote a quick note to Tyler, telling him the news, and addressed it to his dorm at LSU in Baton Rouge. He was also in his freshman year, majoring in business. Though from the one – barely literate – postcard he'd sent that Fall, Tyler seemed to spend most of his time either drunk or hung-over at the DKE house.

It was about ten when George finally dialed Rankin's dormitory. The phone was at the end of a long hall, and it would ring out forever before anyone bothered to pick it up. Eventually I heard him ask for Rankin Calhoun in room 317.

There was another long pause before my brother came to the phone. George skirted around his purpose for as long as possible, asking the usual questions about the poli sci final or Rankin's class standing on his Geology exam. I watched him listen to my brother's reply, nodding with a tense smile, as though Rankin could see him through the phone.

'That's good,' he said, absently. 'I do have some bad news though.'